"THE FUNNIEST DAMN BOOK OF THE YEAR . . . The best way to read it is one installment per week stretched out over a year, but it doesn't work that way. It demands to be read cover to cover."

—SEATTLE POST-INTELLIGENCER

"DON'T MISS THIS PARTY. IT WILL BLOW YOUR MIND . . . You'll meet Harvey and Kate, the main characters, and all their best friends . . . Martha and Bill, who've split after their hip marriage (Martha's fifth) even though they'd signed a contract defining conjugal rights and responsibility for the garbage . . . Carol will be there eying the waiter with the terrific torso; she'll have the butch haircut she got after she decided to come out and come to terms with her homosexual drives . . . Naomi and Jason, of course. They believe in dealing with the whole child, but they probably won't bring John-John, because he spilled scalding coffee down Jason's pants leg and then gave him the finger . . . Marlene, too. She and Kate are terrific friends now since she gave up sex with Harv and joined Kate's consciousness-raising group . . . and Ms. Murphy. She was the one who got Harvey into group sex until his back gave out . . . Really, they all are beautiful people."

To see the way some o . . .
behind and totally com . . .
nationwide sensation, p . . .

"A SUPERFUNNY BOOK . . . FLASH ON *THE SERIAL!* Cyra McFadden knows where you're coming from and has written a fantastically laid-back book you can really get behind and move with. Its incredible insights will blow you away and make it impossible for you to like ever go to another middle-class party until about 1985." —PROVIDENCE JOURNAL

"There it is . . . the unblinking ear and the savage eye and the California 'dynamic' . . . 52 installments in the hipper-than-thou life of Marin County, California, where everybody is supposed to be 'mellow and laid back' even though it's a 'whole high-energy trip with all these happening people.'" —THE NEW YORK TIMES

"Chic, with-it Californians searching for themselves through 'meaningful experiences'—like adultery and TM, consciousness-raising and motorcycles, contractual relationships and weird t-shirts. They are, don't you know, 'going through changes,' constantly and hilariously in a comedy that outhips Mary Hartman." —SAN FRANCISCO EXAMINER

"The wistful transformation of California counter-culture into middle-class angst is savagely charted as McFadden scrutinizes empty lives and even emptier heads. Money-mad bourgeois impulses joust uncomfortably with the good life of the liberated consciousness; the dichotomy is hilariously exposed in incidents which ring true to life and cut close to the bone in an exaggerated travesty of psychic fads and materialistic greed." —BOOKLIST

"IT'S THE FUNNIEST BOOK EVER WRITTEN!"

—Lisa Alther, author of *Kinflicks*

"IT'S HILARIOUS . . . A SOAP OPERA FOR VETERANS OF THE ACID WARS."

—PLAYBOY

" 'Ten years ago, finding out that Kate was getting it on with another man, while not exactly a piece of cake, would have been something Harvey could have handled . . . Now, however, it wasn't that simple. Wife-beating, in Marin in the '70s, was considered a crime against humanity second only to lighting a cigarette in a crowded elevator' . . . AN EXTRAORDINARILY FUNNY BOOK. I MEAN IT'S A REAL TRIP!"

—BOSTON GLOBE

"DELIGHTFUL . . . SCATHING RICH HUMOR . . . Welcome to Marin County where the Grew-Up-Absurd crew subsists on clichés and is wrapped up in brandnames. Welcome to *Serial,* a 52-vignette tour of Plasticland, U.S.A., where getting it together is what's coming down. And it's illustrated. Too much!"

—THE HARTFORD COURANT

Big Bestsellers from SIGNET

☐ **ROGUE'S MISTRESS by Constance Gluyas.**
(#E8339—$2.25)

☐ **SAVAGE EDEN by Constance Gluyas.**
(#E8338—$2.25)

☐ **WOMAN OF FURY by Constance Gluyas.**
(#E8075—$2.25)*

☐ **BEYOND THE MALE MYTH by Anthony Pietro-pinto, M.D., and Jacqueline Simenauer.**
(#E8076—$2.50)

☐ **CRAZY LOVE: An Autobiographical Account of Marriage and Madness by Phyllis Naylor.**
(#J8077—$1.95)

☐ **THE PSYCHOPATHIC GOD: ADOLF HITLER by Robert Waite.**
(#E8078—$2.95)

☐ **THE SWARM by Arthur Herzog.** (#E8079—$2.25)

☐ **TWINS by Bari Wood and Jack Geasland.**
(#E8015—$2.50)

☐ **MARATHON: The Pursuit of the Presidency 1972-1976 by Jules Witcover.**
(#E8034—$2.95)

☐ **THE RULING PASSION by Shaun Herron.**
(#E8042—$2.25)

☐ **CONSTANTINE CAY by Catherine Dillon.**
(#J8307—$1.95)

☐ **WHITE FIRES BURNING by Catherine Dillon.**
(#J8281—$1.95)

☐ **THE WHITE KHAN by Catherine Dillon.**
(#J8043—$1.95)*

☐ **KID ANDREW CODY AND JULIE SPARROW by Tony Curtis.**
(#E8010—$2.25)*

☐ **WINTER FIRE by Susannah Leigh.**
(#E8011—$2.25)*

*Price slightly higher in Canada

If you wish to order these titles,

please see the coupon in

the back of this book.

THE SERIAL

A year in the life of Marin County

by
Cyra McFadden

Illustrations by Tom Cervenak

A SIGNET BOOK

NEW AMERICAN LIBRARY

TIMES MIRROR

NAL BOOKS ARE ALSO AVAILABLE AT DISCOUNTS IN BULK QUANTITY
FOR INDUSTRIAL OR SALES-PROMOTIONAL USE.
FOR DETAILS, WRITE TO
PREMIUM MARKETING DIVISION, NEW AMERICAN LIBRARY, INC.,
1301 AVENUE OF THE AMERICAS, NEW YORK, NEW YORK 10019.

COPYRIGHT © 1976, 1977 BY CYRA McFADDEN

All rights reserved. For information address Alfred A. Knopf, Inc.,
201 East 50th Street, New York, New York 10022.

This is an authorized reprint of an edition published by
Alfred A. Knopf, Inc. Published simultaneously in Canada by
Random House of Canada Limited, Toronto.

Library of Congress Catalog Card Number: 76-47946

Portions of this book originally appeared in the *Pacific Sun*.

SIGNET TRADEMARK REG. U.S. PAT. OFF. AND FOREIGN COUNTRIES
REGISTERED TRADEMARK—MARCA REGISTRADA
HECHO EN CHICAGO, U.S.A.

SIGNET, SIGNET CLASSICS, MENTOR, PLUME AND MERIDIAN BOOKS
are published by The New American Library, Inc.,
1301 Avenue of the Americas, New York, New York 10019

FIRST SIGNET PRINTING, JUNE, 1978

5 6 7 8 9

PRINTED IN THE UNITED STATES OF AMERICA

For Hugh Southern

Contents

[ix]

THE SERIAL

1. Staying mellow in Marin

Once, ten years ago, Marin County had been something they could regard with a mixture of wistfulness and detachment through the haze of smoke at the Buena Vista on Sunday mornings while they drank aquavit and decided where to go for dim sum.

Now they lived in Mill Valley. Not in the house they had in mind when they moved, though: the old canyon house with the view of Mount Tam, the leaded windows, the decks and the immutable Marin ambience—a sunny blend of affluence, redwoods, bohemianism and old golden oak furniture bought for a song on McAllister Street. The realtor had shown them a few houses that fit their lyrical descriptions all those years ago, but they had rapidly learned that they couldn't afford to prop up the sagging foundations, fumigate for scorpions, bring the plumbing up to code and make the necessary structural repairs. In one house they'd seen, which their realtor described as "needing only an infusion of good taste," Kate had put her foot through a hole in the kitchen floor.

So they had settled instead for a tract house on the Sutton Manor flatlands; it was big enough, comfortable and just barely affordable. Besides, the first time they'd seen it, a racing green '63 TR-4 was parked in the driveway, a strong indication that the house's present owners were okay people. If they could live in a tract house, so could Kate and Harvey.

And it was still Marin, though just barely; Kate still hated to tell people, when she gave directions, to stay on East Blithedale all the way out, as if they were heading for 101, turn left at the Chevron station, go past the Red Cart, and turn right at the carwash.

Somehow, in Kate's eyes, the TR-4 had clinched the deal. But although the Harrises had become good friends during the course of the sale because they, too, belonged to the ACLU and the Sierra Club and went to the Mozart Festival at Stolte Grove every year with the picnic of the month from *Sunset* in a Cost Plus hamper, they had taken the TR-4 with them when they moved uphill.

Sometimes Kate wondered if she and Harvey would ever move uphill. Marin Monopoly dictated that every time you made another thou after taxes, you moved and gained another hundred feet in altitude. The Harrises, for example, had made it from a hilltop in Mill Valley to a higher hilltop in San Rafael, and finally, in a pace-setting coup, back to the City, where they lived in a penthouse on Telegraph Hill.

In all that time, Harvey and Kate had never passed Go. Harvey made a lot more money now than he had then, but they spent it rapidly on things they hadn't known existed ten years ago: Rossignol Stratos and season lift tickets at Squaw; twin Motobecane ten-speeds; Kate's Cuisinart, which did *everything* but put the pâté in the oven; Stine graphics; Gumpoldskirchner and St. Émilion (Harvey had "put down" a case in the vacuum cleaner closet); Klip speakers and the top-of-the-line Pioneer receiver; Brown-Jordan patio furniture; Dansk stainless and Rosenthal china; long-stemmed strawberries and walnut oil from the Mill Valley Market; Birkenstock sandals and Adidas (Kate didn't actually jog yet, but she was reading *The Ultimate Athlete*). . . .

The money flowed like wine, and it sometimes seemed to Kate that they could save a lot of time and energy if they just sat down and ate Harvey's paycheck, flamed in brandy, and eliminated most of the middlemen.

The tract house was still big enough (Zero Population Growth, Inc., had become influential shortly after they moved in), and everyone told Kate that after an infusion of good taste, it didn't look like a tract house at all. But it still wasn't the real Marin. For one thing, golden oak looked ridiculous in a tract house, and so did Victorian; they had finally discarded most of their Goodwill goodies.

Now the same pieces, or similar ones, were for sale at stores in downtown Mill Valley that played KKHI on quadraphonic speakers while their proprietors read *The New York Review of Books* at roll-top desks that were to die over. Kate had just priced a lion-footed round oak table at one of these stores, after tracking down the proprietor at Sweetwater. A sign on his door had directed her to look for him there during business hours, which were noon to four on Wednesdays.

Warming the bowl of his wineglass meditatively in the palm of his hand, he had looked over her right ear and quoted her a price of eleven hundred dollars. He had also asked her if she knew what to do for a paranoid Boston fern.

The table would have looked all wrong in their dining nook anyway, and eleven hundred dollars was well beyond their Master Charge limit. But they had to do *something* about their Danish modern expandable, which was in good taste when they bought it but was out, as opposed to "far out," now. Thank God they hadn't bought that chrome-and-glass campaign table six months ago; chrome and glass was out, too, if Kate's friend Carol, who knew about such things because her current old

[4]

man knew the advertising man at *Rolling Stone*, was any anthority.

Carol had been the first woman in their consciousness-raising group, where Kate met her, to wear black fingernail polish. She had just given her own chrome-and-glass campaign table to the Goodwill, which let you fill out your own tax-exemption slip, while Family Service League estimated the value itself.

Thinking about the Danish modern expandable was making Kate tense, and tension, she knew, was bad for you; it led to depression, which was a real downer. The thing to do was to stay mellow at all costs.

She sat back in the Eames chair, forced herself to ignore the roar of Harvey's compost grinder, pounding the split-level and rattling the windows, and concentrated on her mantra until she was feeling laid back again. It was just unbelievable how meditation helped her to organize her priorities.

Her mind wandered, which her TM instructor said was perfectly all right, and she thought about Martha's wedding this afternoon and then about her own wedding, complete with bridesmaids in matching taffeta and her little niece, now into hallucinogens and living on a commune in Taos, as ring-bearer. Weddings were much less conformist now that people were getting behind marriage again; just last weekend, Carol had gone to one filmed live by the Mitchell brothers.

Martha's last wedding had just blown Kate away, so she was looking forward to this one, too. . . .

2. Hip wedding on Mount Tam

As she got ready for Martha's wedding, Kate reflected happily that one great thing about living in Marin was that your friends were always growing and changing. She couldn't remember, for example, how many times Martha had been married before.

She wondered if she ought to call her friend Carol and ask what to wear. Martha had said "dress down," but that could mean anything from Marie Antoinette milkmaid from The Electric Poppy to bias-cut denims from Moody Blues. Kate didn't have any bias-cut denims, because she'd been waiting to see how long they'd stay in, but she could borrow her adolescent daughter's. They wore the same clothes all the time.

Her husband, Harvey, was already in the shower, so Kate decided on her Renaissance Faire costume. She always felt mildly ridiculous in it, but it wasn't so bad without the conical hat and it was definitely Mount Tam wedding. Now the problem was Harvey, who absolutely refused to go to Mount Tam weddings in the French jeans Kate had bought him for his birthday. She knew he'd wear his Pierre Cardin suit, which was fine two years ago but which was now establishment; and when he came out of the shower, her fears were confirmed.

Since they were already late, though, there was no point in trying to do something about Harvey. They drove up Panoramic to the mountain meadow trying to remember what Martha's bridegroom's name was this time (Harvey thought it was Bill again, but Kate was reasonably sure it wasn't) and made it to the ceremony just as the recorder player, a bare-chested young man perched faunlike on a rock above the assembled guests, began to improvise variations on the latest Pink Floyd.

Right away, Kate spotted Carol and knew her Renaissance dress was all right— marginal, but all right. Carol was wearing Marie Antoinette milkmaid, but with her usual infallible chic, had embellished it with her trademark jewelry: an authentic squash-blossom necklace, three free-form rings bought from a creative artisan at the Mill Valley Art Festival on her right hand, and her old high school charm bracelet updated with the addition of a tiny silver coke spoon.

Reverend Spike Thurston, minister of the Radical Unitarian Church in Terra Linda and active in the Marin Sexual Freedom League, was presiding. Kate was thrilled as the ceremony began and Thurston raised a solemn, liturgical hand; she really got off on weddings.

"Fellow beings," Thurston began, smiling, "I'm not here today as a minister but as a member of the community. Not just the community of souls gathered here, not just the community of Mill Valley, but the larger human community which is the cosmos.

"I'm not going to solemnize this marriage in the usual sense of the word. I'm not going to pronounce it as existing from this day forward. Because nobody can do that except Martha and"—he held a quick, worried conference with somebody behind him—"and Bill."

Harvey was already restless. "Do we have to go to a reception after this thing?" he asked too loudly.

"Organic," Kate whispered, digging her fingernails into his wrist. "At Davood's."

Harvey looked dismayed.

"These children have decided to recite their own vows," Thurston continued. Kate thought "children" was overdoing it a little; Martha was at least forty, although everybody knew chronological age didn't matter these days. "They're not going to recite something after me, because this is a *real* wedding—the wedding of two separate-nesses, two solitarinesses, under the sky."

Thurston pointed out the sky and paused while a jet thundered across it. Kate thought he looked incredibly handsome with his head thrown back and his purple Marvin Gaye T-shirt emblazoned with "Let's Get It On" stretched tightly across his chest.

"Martha," he said, "will you tell us what's in your heart?"

Standing on tiptoe, Kate could just catch a glimpse of the bride; slightly to the right of her, she spotted Martha's ex-husband-once-removed with his spacy new old lady, who, Kate thought, looked like Martha. She tried to remember which of Martha's children, all present and looking oddly androgynous in velvet Lord Fauntleroy suits, were also his.

Martha recited a passage on marriage "from the Spanish poet Federico García Lorca." Last time she was married, she'd said "Frederico." Kate thought the fact that Martha had got it right this time was a good sign; and she adored the Lorca.

When Bill recited in turn, he was almost inaudible, but Kate thought she recognized *The Prophet*, which was *not* a good sign. She dug her fingernails into Harvey again; he was shifting his feet restlessly. This wasn't a sign of anything, necessarily, since Harvey simply couldn't get used to his new Roots, but it was best to be safe.

"Hey, listen," she whispered to Carol, who had wiggled her way through the crowd and was now at her side. "It's terrific, isn't it?"

"Really," Carol whispered back. "He

looks good. He's an architect that does
mini-parks. She met him at her creative
divorce group."

Kate leaned across her to take in the
crowd. She thought she recognized Mimi
Fariña. She also noticed Larry, her shampoo
person from Rape of the Locks, who always
ran her through the soul handshake when
she came in for a cut and blow-dry. She
hoped she wouldn't have to shake hands
with Larry at the reception, since she never
got the scissors/paper/rock maneuvers of the
soul handshake just right and since she was
pretty sure that Larry kept changing it on
her, probably out of repressed racial
animosity.

Thurston, after a few remarks about the
ecology, had just pronounced Martha and

her new husband man and woman. Kate felt
warmly sentimental as the bride and
bridegroom kissed passionately, and loos-
ened her grip on Harvey's wrist. She
noticed that the fog was beginning to lift
slightly and gazed off into the distance.

"Hey, look," she said to Harvey excitedly.
"Isn't that the ocean?"

"The Pacific," Harvey replied tersely.
"Believed to be the largest on the West
Coast. It's part of the cosmos."

Kate felt put down. Harvey was becoming
increasingly uptight these days, and remarks like this one were more frequent.
Look at the way he'd baited her TA instructor at the Brennans' the other night. "You
are not O.K.," he had told him loudly,
lurching slightly in his Roots. "I could give
you a lot of reasons; but take my word for
it—you are *not* O.K."

Yes, Kate was going to have to do
something about Harvey. . . .

3. A visit to the vet's

A week later, Kate was still brooding over her husband Harvey's inscrutable behavior at Martha's wedding reception, where he had managed to offend just about everybody.

Harvey had turned down both the lentil loaf and the hash that was going around the room with a flat pronouncement that hash was illegal and lentil loaf ought to be. He had told several people who asked that his sign was the Mill Valley–East Blithedale turnoff. Finally, he had split entirely for an hour, only to reappear muttering darkly that the Old Mill Tavern had turned into "some kind of goddamn fern bar."

Kate wished that her friend Carol would finish doing Harvey's chart, for while some of his recent aberrations were typically Scorpio and therefore not his fault, she was beginning to suspect he had something weird she didn't know about on the cusp.

Just last night, for instance, over her favorite cassoulet out of "Julia 2," Kate had mentioned casually that she was interested in primal screaming and that she also thought she'd like to get rolfed. Harvey had said he figured if she got rolfed hard enough, she'd scream primally; he had then laughed so hard at his own feeble wit that he'd choked on his *saucisson*.

Nobody could call Kate humorless. She never missed *Doonesbury* or *The Now People* and prized her "Marcel Proust Was a Yenta" button. But she couldn't relate to Harvey's idea of what was funny these days. *No way.*

Her first impulse was to talk things over with her women's group, but the sisters weren't invariably as supportive as she'd hoped they'd be. Kate was still dealing with their reaction a few weeks ago when she'd mentioned that she'd like to take assertiveness training but was afraid Harvey wouldn't let her.

She was on her way to the Redwoode Veterinary Hospital, where she was going to leave her Manx, Kat Vonnegut, Jr., for a flea bath, when it suddenly occurred to her that maybe the answer to her dissatisfactions with Harvey was to get it on with somebody else. She just flashed on it: for once in her life, she ought to put her own needs right up front and then get behind them.

She parked out in back of the Redwoode, where the vets hid their Mercedes 230 SL's, and extricated Kat Vonnegut, thumping around truculently in his cat carrier, from the rear of her VW bus. The hospital was expensive—it cost more to walk through the front door than it did for an office call to their family physician—but Kate was loyal to it because Dr. Gelt had been so terrifically nice to her during Felix Frankfurter's final illness.

Not only had he encouraged her to come down and say goodbye to Felix just before he underwent what the computerized bill later designated "EUTH & DISP," but he had also encouraged her warmly to "have another cat right away," pointing out wisely that they wouldn't want to raise their Afghan, Donald Barthelme, as an only animal.

Anyway, because Mill Valley still had that real small-town atmosphere, she always met a lot of friends in the waiting room. First Peter, who taught a very popular course in "Participatory Salad Making" at Heliotrope, appeared with his Irish setter. Peter had brought Panama Red in for a checkup because when he'd put his mood ring on the dog, just for a joke, it had turned black.

Then Julie, a former neighbor who had made it and moved up to Eldridge, came in to pick up Fanne Foxe Terrier, who had recently been raped, Julie explained, by a dachshund on a macho trip.

Julie had been the only other woman on the block who was heavily into macramé, and Kate missed her and the raps they'd had on lazy summer afternoons while they sat out on Julie's patio tying knots in plant hangers. She told Julie how she felt that life in a technocracy interfered with interpersonal relationships, and Julie agreed. "For sure," she said forcefully. "Do you know how busy I've been lately? I haven't even read the last three issues of *Harper's. That's* how busy I've been."

Eventually the orderly came to get Kat Vonnegut, and Kate went about her rounds. She stopped at Phillips for some Chemex filters and her own special blend of Madagascar, Senegalese and caffeine-free French roast, picked up a copy of *Zen and the Art of Motorcycle Maintenance* for her eight-year-old nephew's birthday, and wound up at the Mill Valley Market, which was swarming with female tennis players.

You couldn't run around downtown Mill Valley in a bikini, which was tacky, but tennis dresses were socially acceptable anywhere. The tennis types tromped through the MVM in impeccable crotch-length whites, their deeply tanned legs flashing, little half moons of exposed white buttock glimmering as they leaned into the dairy cases for kefir, and the tassels that kept their socks up bobbing like cottontails at their heels. Kate, who hadn't signed up in time for membership in the Scott Valley Tennis Club, was deeply envious.

But her mind wasn't really on threads; she had definitely decided, maybe while she was buying WD-40 for Harvey's com-

post grinder at Varney's, to take a lover. Now the question was whose.

Just a few years ago, the husbands in her peer group had stroked her bare spine when she wore her backless black cocktail dress to parties and told her that she figured spectacularly in their dream lives. Now they were liberated; all the men she knew who had propositioned her had long since apologized and told her that they really, *really* respected her as a person. And of course she wouldn't be caught dead at a party anymore dressed as a sex symbol.

Poking kumquats and wondering if Harvey would eat jicama, Kate ran down the list of men she knew; they turned up rejects one after another, until she remembered Leonard. A psychologist specializing in the dysfunctional socialization of rich children,

Leonard had an office in Tiburon, a reputation as a stud, and the warm, spontaneous personality of a true Sagittarius. He also had a lot of curly black chest hair which he displayed by wearing his shirts unbuttoned to the belly button.

Kate wasn't really high on chest hair because it seemed to collect deviled egg and little globs of hummus at stand-up parties. But Leonard had a lot going for him otherwise, and Kate liked the space he was in. Besides, she couldn't think of anyone else, since most of the men she knew, if not married, were at least committed to an LTR ("living together relationship").

And so, reminding herself nervously that there was no such thing as guilt, she paid for her kumquats, got into the bus and headed for Tiburon. . . .

4. Leonard as a lover

Kate's attempt to take her psychiatrist friend
Leonard as a lover couldn't have turned out
worse if Sam Peckinpah had written her life
script. But it looked great in the planning
stage, while she was still conceptualizing it,
and she trucked off to Tiburon that awful
day in a warm glow of anticipation. She was
feeling just terrific. For one thing, she was
wearing her new proletarian-chic overalls,
which were dynamite. For another, she had
decided to play the whole scene off the
wall, to just go with the flow. Everybody
knew, in these days of heightened consciousness, that the rational mind was a
screw-up; the really authentic thing to do
was to act on your impulses.

How could she have dreamed that two
hours later she'd be gorging compulsively
on refined sugar at the Swedish bakery,
weeping into her coffee, and wondering
how to get even with Leonard for doing that
absolutely unbelievable number on her?

Omens and portents were everywhere, if
she'd just stopped to notice them. For one
thing, Tiburon was crawling with tourist
types, in drip-dry coordinates, and their no-

class wives, who all looked like runners-up for Miss Disneyland of 1955. For another, when she finally found a parking place in front of Tiburon Vintners, another VW bus tried to back into it while she was backing and filling.

Kate won, but not before the other driver, whose bumper sticker read "One World, One Spirit, One Humanity," had given her the finger. Then she got the pant leg of her overalls caught in the bus door, a blow because they were just back from Meader's. Kate hadn't dared wash them because she was afraid the Esso patch would run.

And finally, when she got to Leonard's office in the back of a remodeled ark he shared with a head shop, Sunshine, Leonard's receptionist, was still at her desk. Kate had hoped she'd be off on her yogurt break.

At last Sunshine padded out in her beaded moccasins, made for her "by this native American craftsman who's one thirty-second Cherokee," and Kate stopped pretending to read *Psychology Today* and restlessly paced Leonard's office, which was wittily decorated with positively Jungian primitive African masks and a collection of shrunken heads.

Leonard emerged from his inner sanctum a few minutes later escorting a boy of about seven. The boy was carrying something Kate recognized, incredulously, as one of those plastic dog messes from the sidewalk stands in Chinatown. As she stared, he thrust it at Leonard.

"Nummy num num!" Leonard said enthusiastically, pretending to take a bite. Then he steered the kid out the door a bit more firmly than seemed absolutely necessary. "And remember," he told him, waving, "stay loose."

Kate couldn't help blowing her cool and asking what *that* was all about, and when Leonard told her that Kevin had "this mind and body dichotomy thing," and that Leonard was trying to get him in touch with himself, starting with feces, her throat closed.

So they got off to a bad start, and things went steadily downhill from there. Kate suggested lunch, but they couldn't agree where to go; she liked El Burro, but Leonard was "enchilada'd out" and had also "O.D.'d on tostadas compuestas" the night before. He manipulated her into agreeing on Sam's Deck, which Kate didn't like because the last time she'd gone there, a gull had dumped on her shrimp Louie.

Worst of all, when they were sitting on the sunny deck at last, he couldn't stop talking about his own trip, rapping at her in this very hyper way about how he was into corporal punishment, the latest breakthrough in child psychology. He said he'd had amazing results just acting out his anger with his patients. He was also big on video feedback ("fantastic"), role-playing ("fantastic") and Japanese hot tubs, which made meaningful human interaction "practically inevitable."

Her anxieties mounting as Leonard ordered another Wallbanger (did she have enough cash in her Swedish carpenter's tool kit to cover the tab?), Kate wondered how a man who had spent three weekends at Esalen and knew Werner Erhard personally could be so insensitive. She kept trying to tell Leonard about Harvey's hangups and how repressed she was because of them, but Leonard wouldn't really pay attention. Although he kept saying, "I hear you, I hear you," he wasn't listening, and once, when she confessed a particularly intimate dissatisfaction with Harvey, he murmured absently, *"That's* cool. . . ."

Her self-image disintegrating rapidly, Kate decided to lay her body on the line. "Leonard," she said, raising her voice, "I'm sorry to dump on you like this, but I'm on a really heavy trip right now, you know? Like, I can't get my act together." She paused significantly. "Leonard, I *need* you. I want you to help me get clear."

Leonard leaned across the table and gave Kate his full attention for the first time. At least she thought he did; he was wearing acid glasses, so it was hard to tell.

"Listen," he said sincerely, "I know exactly where you're coming from." He covered her hand warmly with his, crushing the piece of hamburger bun she'd been nervously shredding.

"Why don't you come to my place in Bolinas for the weekend?" His turquoise ring bit into her knuckles as he began to chant seductively. "Wholistic nutrition ... hypnosis ... biofeedback ... massage ..." Kate was beginning to hyperventilate when he added, in another voice entirely, "Friday night through Sunday noon. One hundred and fifty bucks if you crash in the dorm. Extra charge for the hot tub. I take Master Charge, American Express, all your major credit cards."

Kate had seldom felt such overwhelming affection for her husband, good old Harvey, as she did when she was back in her Mill Valley tract house that afternoon, cooking her nuclear family a gourmet dinner to expiate her guilt and wondering how she could manage to plant a dead horse in Leonard's waterbed. But while she was furiously mashing chicken livers, which reminded her unpleasantly of Kevin's plastic turd, Harvey called to say he wouldn't be home for dinner and not to wait up.

She knew better, of course, but she felt an alarming little pang of suspicion. The fourth time this week, and was Harvey really *that* far behind on his flow charts?

5. Harvey takes a turn

As Kate half suspected, Harvey was lying when he called to tell her he was working late that night. An hour after he left the Market and Montgomery main office of Wells Fargo, where he was an escrow officer, Harvey was sitting in the garden patio of the *no name* drinking Tequila Sunrises and brooding about his marriage, his fortieth birthday a few weeks ago, and the larger subject of "life."

He was also doing some heavy thinking about his secretary, Ms. Murphy, whom he'd been avidly trying to seduce since she rose majestically out of the typing pool, like Venus rising from whatever it was she rose from, the December before. This week alone, Harvey had managed to get her to a five o'clock retrospective of *Behind the Green Door* (Monday night), to the White Horse for drinks (Tuesday night), and to a five-martini lunch at Paoli's (Wednesday noon). He hadn't, however, managed to get her into bed.

Ms. Murphy shared a three-room pad at the Portofino Riviera Adult Apartments, in Sausalito, with two stewardesses. Harvey kept track of their flight schedules as efficiently as he kept track of the bank's money and so had known, when Ms. Murphy asked him to drive her home tonight, that one of the stews was at the airport and the other forty thousand feet over Wichita. Foolishly, he'd let himself speculate that tonight was the night.

But Ms. Murphy had hopped out the passenger side of his sedate Volvo sedan a few minutes ago with the agility of a Chinese acrobat, calling over her shoulder her thanks for the lift and an uninflected "Keep on truckin." Apparently she wasn't a banker groupie.

He should have known. When he'd interviewed Ms. Murphy all those months ago, she had told him succinctly that (1) she wasn't "into making coffee for the head honcho"; (2) she thought taking shorthand "from some MCP with a big desk" one more variation on the master-slave relationship; and (3) she "couldn't get behind one-hour lunch breaks."

Harvey had winced and hired her. First of all, he wasn't a male chauvinist pig, God forbid, and secondly, Ms. Murphy had succulent thighs beneath the long Levi's skirt she buttoned just enough to keep it from falling off. Employing her seemed like a perfect opportunity to do well by doing good.

But Ms. Murphy had proven as difficult

and inscrutable as Kate and his daughter Joan, both of whom had become so hypersensitive to "anti-feminist put-downs" in the last year that they oinked at him, in concert, just about every time he opened his mouth. The other night, for instance, Kate had asked him to go to a "Rich Radicals for Tom Hayden" rally in Kentfield. Since they'd already been to three of these, Harvey thought the prospect was a bummer, but he agreed because, he said, there was always the chance that Jane Fonda would be there in a miniskirt.

Kate had immediately reclaimed her "Uppity Women Unite" button from the silver chest and pinned it conspicuously to the bib of her overalls, while Joan, whose abuse of the language sometimes offended Harvey more acutely than her flaming adolescent contempt for him and the establishment he represented, had told him that she had "never heard anything so gross in my whole life, practically."

Harvey had agreed in principle that he didn't think Jane Fonda's legs were a joke, but he was still burned.

Ogling the *no name* waitress, who signaled subtly just by the way she plonked down his complimentary plate of raw vegetables and California dip that she knew all about him and his kind, Harvey wondered whatever happened to Baby Jane Fonda? Whatever happened to his wife,

Kate, who had once spent happy afternoons starching the kitchen curtains and baking chocolate chip cookies for the Edna Maguire PTA but was now obsessed with the real human being she might have been if he hadn't consigned her to a life of cleaning out toilet bowls with Jonny Mops? What the hell had happened to *women*?

Harvey believed in equal pay for equal work; he did his share of the chores for his and Kate's dinner parties by choosing the wine and reminding her to make ice; he hired Ms. Murphy, even though she typed thirty words a minute and spelled "Fargo" with an *e* on the end, because any woman with thighs like hers deserved a chance to make it. But what had his egalitarianism got him? Nothing for Frank Harris to write his memoirs about.

Full of injured merit and tequila, Harvey paid his tab, tipped the uppity waitress the pittance she deserved, and strolled out into the balmy evening, still sober enough to plan his next move and to two-step neatly through the ankle-deep accumulation of assorted sidewalk crud on picturesque Bridgeway. He was headed for The Trident, where he dimly supposed the action was on a Thursday night in Marvelous Marin, but he couldn't help pausing to browse in the lighted window of The Upstart Crow for words to live by. *The Silenced Majority, Up Against the Wall, Mother* and *Shoulder to*

Shoulder. Harvey groaned. When Kate had finished *Women and Madness* recently, she hadn't spoken to him, except when she had to, for a week and a half.

The Trident looked a little more like it. Harvey pushed his way through the bodies, propped himself against the bar and took in the whole gestalt: bra-less waitresses rising and falling gently with the tide; rock band managers in narrow-waisted white suits straight out of *Heart of Darkness* scarfing up brown rice and veggies; "Journey" reverberating off the tie-dyed ceiling. It was a mellow scene.

Harvey pulled his shades out of his pocket and unobtrusively stroked his modified Prince Valiant—which had cost him a bundle at Spiderman Hair Design but had changed his whole image—with the small natural-bristle brush he always carried. His fortieth birthday was beginning to recede into the slush that was his pre-California existence, the gray area in his past before he learned about papayas, patchouli oil and the sexual revolution. Beside him, a woman in a silver body stocking from Mom's Apple Grave and eight-inch platforms that reminded him of the moon shot was telling a friend about the progress of her affair with someone named Hughie. "I dunno how it's all gonna come out," she said. "It's all very murky, y'know? He's flown to London for the weekend to try to get his head together."

Through the artificial gloom of his shades, and while he was still trying to assimilate this particular bit of input, Harvey saw an apparition. There, under the second fern from the right, looking incredibly foxy in a feather boa from The Painted Lady, sat his very own secretary, Ms. Murphy, lugubriously stirring her carrot juice with her right forefinger. She was alone.

Harvey couldn't believe it, but Ms. Murphy was for real; he picked up his drink, slouching into his best approximation of cool, and headed toward her. Maybe tonight *was* the night. . . .

6. Assault on Ms. Murphy

Harvey had a slight edge going for him the night he decided to pick up his secretary, Ms. Murphy, at The Trident, where he had spotted her all alone. Ms. Murphy was feeling bummed out because the guy she was waiting for, an artist who was heavily into belt-buckle casting, hadn't made the scene. So she welcomed Harvey warmly if warily, and shortly consented to leave with him for other voices, other rooms.

They started out at Agatha Pubb's, where Harvey persuaded her to abandon carrot juice for Dos Equis, moved on to an instant replay back at the *no name,* and were sitting cozily thigh to thigh at the Sausalito Food Company several hours later, discussing sheep symbolism in Ingmar Bergman (Ms. Murphy was "a film freak"), when she proposed that they raise their blood sugar levels with dinner at The French Restaurant in San Rafael.

Harvey had never been to The French Restaurant, although everybody told him the food was outasight, and wondered uneasily if he'd meet anybody he knew there. He also wondered if the joint took credit cards, since he was running through what was left of his allowance, doled out by Kate on Monday morning, at an alarming rate.

But Ms. Murphy's warm breath was stimulating an erogenous zone he hadn't even known he had, his right earlobe, as she told him that she could really dig *quenelles* about now. So he decided to hang loose and risk it.

Harvey called for a reservation from the Food Company pay phone, contemplating the prospect of plying Ms. Murphy with Château Lafite-Rothschild and then whisking her, well-fed and grateful, home to her own little bed. Assured by a voice with a fruity accent at the other end that The French Restaurant would have *"un intime leetle table for two"* waiting for him in half an hour, he hit 101 like the winner of the last Monte Carlo Grand Prix, trying to remember to say "films" instead of "movies" and to come on like the serious cineaste he might have been if he didn't fall asleep, inevitably, during second features at the Surf.

Ms. Murphy was telling him how *Scenes from a Marriage* had just simply devastated, once and for all, the whole institutionalized gestalt that kept people from really, *really* relating to each other on your basic, honest human level, when he maneuvered his Volvo into the last slot in the parking lot, between a Porsche 911 and a Citröen

Maserati. "Like, would your wife let you fart in the living room?" she asked him intensely. "Or would you have to blame it on the dog or something?"

Stunned, Harvey said after a pause that he was really glad she'd asked him that question because it really made him *think*. This seemed to be the right response; Ms. Murphy clung amorously to his arm as they walked into the dim interior of The French Restaurant, and whispered to him, just as the door closed behind them, that she thought he was really a beautiful human being.

Pierre, whose fame as the proprietor *de maison* was county-wide, swooped down on them out of the darkness immediately. "Ah, M'sieur Holroyd," he cried. "How *charmant!* And your *femme ... chicalors!*" He seized Ms. Murphy's hand and began to smother it with audible kisses. "Madame, thees ees too much. I am ovairwhelm. For my humble establishment you wear ze colors of ze French *tricolor!*"

Ms. Murphy fondled her boa and seemed to melt into a little puddle at Pierre's neat, Gucci-clad feet, but Harvey was moved only to pat his wallet anxiously. He was pretty sure all that Gallic charm didn't come cheap.

And once they were seated at the *intime* leetle table, he realized bleakly that he was way out of his depth for sure. The French

Restaurant was full of doctors. Doctors to the right of them, doctors to the left of them. Into the valley of debt. The doctors were ordering the Château Lafite Harvey had decided against after one quick squint at the wine list, reminding the wine steward to "let it breathe, Jean-Louis" and discussing malpractice insurance.

"What really gets me about the whole schmeer," said one of their wives to another, dissecting her duck with surgical precision, "is what's gonna happen to the doctor-patient relationship. Herb is a human being, too. He can't exactly keep his mind on somebody's liver when he's worrying all the time about how we're gonna make the next payment on the condo at Incline."

Pierre, meanwhile, was diving and swooping around Harvey's and Ms. Murphy's table, recommending the rack of lamb, which he could humbly assure them was "supairb" this evening, *exactement à point.* The rack of lamb was also $37.50 for two, à la carte, and Harvey's heart sank when Ms. Murphy said she thought it sounded fantastic and why didn't they just leave the whole number up to Pierre?

Harvey was afraid the whole number, left to Pierre, was going to be equivalent to the down payment on a cabin cruiser.

Finally, on the pretense of going to the men's room, he left Ms. Murphy with her apéritif, steeled himself, approached Pierre behind the bar and asked him if The French Restaurant took credit cards. Through the redolent steam from the kitchen, Pierre regarded him as if Harvey were a high-ranking German officer goose-stepping down the Champs-Élysées during the occupation of Paris. He said stonily that he considered credit cards "déclassé" but would accept M'sieur's personal "cheque" if M'sieur was temporarily short of spot cash money.

That tore it. Writing a check was out. Kate kept the household accounts, and no way could Harvey explain a rack of lamb for two, however *à point*, on a Thursday night when he was supposed to be working late at the bank. With no other viable alternatives, he returned to the table, screwed his face into an approximation of acute pain, and told Ms. Murphy that it really freaked him out to do this but that his back had just gone out and they had to leave immediately. He said it quietly in case a lower back specialist at the next table overheard him.

Ms. Murphy went. But not quietly. She tore into him all the way to Sausalito, slammed his car door in his face for the second time that night, and left with a parting shot that he was just the kind of hypocritical creepo Ingmar Bergman was trying to stamp out.

The Volvo rattled, all the way back to Mill Valley, with the cartonful of bottles

Harvey was supposed to have taken to the recycling depot in the Tam High parking lot the weekend before. It seemed to him, through an alcoholic buzz, that his goddamn car was laughing at him; but he felt better when he pulled into the tract house driveway and saw lights blazing inside. His own dear wife, who didn't think Ingmar Bergman had it in for him personally, was waiting up for him. Maybe she'd even make him a fried egg sandwich.

But the scene which greeted him inside, a hip version of a Breughel print, wasn't the one he'd been anticipating. . . .

7. Joan's scene

Harvey came home from his Waterloo at The French Restaurant that night to find his living room transformed into a mini-Winterland: Alice Cooper thundering out of the stereo, the brush-fire smell of pot heavy in the air, and a mass of writhing bodies, from which issued an occasional cryptic cry of "Get down!"

Apparently his daughter Joan had taken seriously their recent parental injunction to bring her friends home instead of whiling away the best years of her life crusing Fourth Street.

At least the writhing bodies were writhing more or less upright. Harvey peered through the smoke, arranged what he thought was a serenely together smile on his face, and resolved not to give off negative vibes. It was important, according to the family therapist they'd consulted a few times at Rites of Passage, to "keep the lines of communication open."

He didn't see Joan right away or at least didn't recognize her. Like all her peers, Joan wore her hair long, straight and parted in the middle, and was dressed like one of those waifs that made Harvey so uneasy when he chuckled over the *New Yorker* cartoons once a week: "You can save little Ming Lee or you can turn the page." Harvey knew he ought to save little Ming Lee, and one of these days he'd get around to sending off a check; in the meantime, he didn't appreciate *The New Yorker*'s giving him only the two choices.

He did spot Joan's boyfriend Spenser. Harvey was also uneasy about Spenser, a high school dropout with no visible means of livelihood and the only Ferrari Harvey had ever seen this side of *La Dolce Vita*. But Kate kept telling him not to make "value judgments," a form of human error she equated with child-beating or rolling drunks. So he was careful not to verbalize his suspicions that the reason Spenser went to Jamaica every few months was not, as Joan assured him, deadpan, that he was "heavily into reggae."

"Oh, hi there, man," Spenser said vaguely, when Harvey made his way to him. "How's everything at Market and Montgomery? You taking good care of capitalism?"

Harvey looked at Spenser. Wasp Afro, puka shells, Che Guevara T-shirt. Joan thought Spenser was "a fox"; Harvey thought he was a weasel. "Listen," he said, "what's going on here?" Spenser stared at him blankly. "I mean, what's going down?"

"Oh. Yeah." Spenser thought for a long time and then smiled beatifically. "Like, you know, man. Whatever's right. Just a few of the freaks, can you dig it?"

Harvey decided that Spenser's lines of communication were permanently down. He thought of Spenser's brain as the welter of tangled multicolored wires that came out of the wall when the telephone serviceman came to work on the intercom at the bank. "Where's Joan?" he asked, articulating carefully.

"She's in a good space, man," Spenser said. He suddenly suffered what looked like a major muscle spasm but was just Alice Cooper getting through to him. "Aw-*right!*" Spenser screamed.

Harvey finally found his daughter and her

friend Anita in the kitchen, calmly grazing in the lettuce bin of the refrigerator, but not before he had registered the presence of a sinister-looking Harley chopper in the family room behind them. "Whose god-damn bike is that?" he asked.

Joan looked at him, alfalfa sprouts trailing out the corners of her mouth, as if he had a communicable disease. She usually looked at him that way. "It's Michael's," she said. "Anita's new old man. And get off my case."

Anita nodded, smiling sweetly. "Could you relate to a carrot?" she asked him.

"Why did he bring it into the house?" Harvey was trying not to bellow, because Joan had complained that he always bellowed at her, and their therapist had said he shouldn't do that unless it was the only way he really felt natural.

"It's valuable."

"It's leaving an oil slick on the floor."

"You want it to get ripped off? Michael needs it. Like he *commutes* on it."

"Michael's got a gig at the Discowreck in San Rafael," Anita put in. "You been to the Discowreck?"

"I don't want it in my house," Harvey shouted. He couldn't help himself. "Do you know how many years it took us to convert that garage into a family room? What do you think it is, a goddamn garage?"

"Listen," Anita said. "Don't *worry*, okay? Michael's gonna turn it in on a Cessna and take flying lessons. He says he's had it with the ground."

Spenser, meanwhile, had appeared in the doorway. "You got any bread, man?" he asked Harvey, with the same loony smile.

"Filthy capitalist money, Spenser?" Harvey said nastily. "I thought you didn't touch the stuff."

"Aw, no, man." Spenser rolled his eyes heavenward, appealing to a higher authority for patience. "No, you know. Bread. For toast. Like, I could really munch out on toast, man. You know? Toast and jelly?"

In the middle of this exchange, Kate came in, beaming. "Well," she said happily. "Isn't this nice?"

Harvey restrained himself.

Kate began to tell Joan excitedly about this great book report they'd heard at her consciousness-raising group, her regular Thursday-night outing, on *How to Say No to a Rapist and Survive.*

"How do you get the guy to back off?" Anita asked.

"Well," Kate said, "the first thing is you don't get upset. You *reason* with him."

Harvey looked over Kate's head at the gleaming chopper, which terrified him. Hell's Angels . . . *Scorpio Rising.* "Listen," he said. "I want everybody out." When Spenser stared at him uncomprehendingly again, he added vehemently, *"Split!"*

And slowly, they did, though it took

Michael quite a while to wheel the chopper around and get it out the family room door again. "Like, it doesn't reverse, man," he told Harvey. "It's not like a fucking car or something."

"Harvey, how could you?" Kate asked, when Joan had gone noisily down the hall, screaming at Harvey about how he was a "sickie on a power trip." "It's her *scene*. She's got a different lifestyle."

A few weeks and many recriminations later, his nuclear family having detonated, Harvey had an entirely different lifestyle, too. . . .

8. Harvey moves out

Harvey was lucky. When he moved out of the tract house at the beginning of his trial separation from Kate, he found a terrific crash pad right away, a one-bedroom condo on Eliseo Drive overlooking the Greenbrae canal. The place belonged to Chuck, a former operations manager at the bank who had "dropped out of the rat race" and was now into bonsai trees, meditation and Zen jogging.

Chuck was off to India for six months to check out an ashram. He left Harvey watering instructions for the bonsai, a few Cost Plus meditation mats and some serious advice: "Cut out the nine-to-five shit, Harv. You gotta get in touch with the universe. That's the first step."

Harvey wondered what the second step was. He couldn't cut out the nine-to-five shit anyway, because he now had two households to support (Kate was selling her macramé at the Marin City flea market Saturday mornings, but the take was just enough to keep her in string) and the condo wasn't cheap. For a mystic, Chuck retained a hard-nosed materialistic streak.

But he still felt he'd made all the right moves. He and Kate had been married to each other longer than any other couple they knew, which certainly suggested some sort of fixated, mutual-dependency thing. And both of them agreed they needed "space," though a one-bedroom condo didn't accord Harvey much of it.

Anyway, he was among friends, or at least equals. Everybody else in the condo was divorced or separated, too, and Harvey had some heavy conversations the first few weeks, steaming in the sauna with his neighbors, about the causes of their respective marital woes. "My wife kept telling me she wanted an open marriage," one of them told him, "and finally I said the subject was closed."

During the same period, Harvey haunted the bar at The Refectory, where, someone had told him—erroneously—the action was. He also spent some time furnishing the condo, having learned rapidly that meditation mats were lousy for Monday-night football on the tube, and felt somewhat more settled when he had run a hose from the bathtub and filled the Innerspace waterbed that signaled his emergence as a liberated man. He'd taken few things from the house, because he and Kate battled so furiously over every object he tried to pack: who'd bought the copy of *The Best and the Brightest* neither of them had got around to reading? Why should he take the Ansel Adams coffee-table book if he didn't have a coffee table?

Then, when he was really beginning to feel sorry for himself, things began to click the way he'd fantasized they would: Marlene moved in. She just came home with him from the Bon Air Road Safe-way one night and stayed.

Harvey had got to know Marlene as she checked out his groceries, expressing horror at "the garbage" he put in "his one and only body." "Do you know what white flour does to you?" she asked him, handing the loaf of bread he'd picked out to a stockboy, to go back on the shelf. *It kills your enzymes.* Marlene, who was eighteen and a part-time ceramics student at the College of Marin, was seriously into nutrition. But since she was also seriously into sex, and since her interest in his one and only body turned out to be virtually limitless, Harvey ate his kelp and drank his soya milk without complaint. If the meals Marlene served him were rare and strange, so were the things she did to him afterward on the waterbed. Harvey was beginning to feel he'd got in touch with the universe.

His only real pang about the whole arrangement was that Marlene introduced him to her friends as her "old man" and complained that he didn't introduce her to his friends at all. Was he ashamed of her

or something? On the contrary. Harvey decided to show her off; he ordered a couple of cases of Fetzer Cabernet Sauvignon, his most recent little-winery find, and invited a few friends in for "wine, cheese and a good rap."

The Sunday afternoon of his coming-out party, Harvey looked around his living room and felt really good about himself for the first time in years; the gathering was a resounding success, even if friends he hadn't seen for a while kept confusing Marlene, who'd unfortunately elected to wear her old Redwood High majorette boots, with his daughter Joan.

In one corner Harriet Sternum, a volunteer at the Audubon Ranch two days a week, had collected quite a crowd, who were listening to her describe the mating habits of blue herons, or as she put it, "how blue herons do it." In another, some Mill Valley friends were heatedly arguing the live-music-down-town issue, with Jerry from the car pool contending that the real problem was the Human Rights Commission, which seemed to believe in human rights mainly for hippies with amplifiers.

Carol, Kate's flaky friend from her consciousness-raising group, was huddled with Leonard, the Tiburon psychologist. Harvey had invited Carol because when he'd run into her in the produce section of the Golden Valley Market, where Marlene had sent him in search of organic fiber, Carol had said she wanted him to know that while she loved Kate, she loved him, too. She and Leonard were rapping about how mesc made you realize that linear thinking was a total shuck. "Harv," Carol asked him, "don't you think Carlos Castaneda really has his act together?"

In the kitchen, a small, rapt group was sniffing cocaine. Marlene was among them, looking a little worried. She didn't believe in sniffing coke, which irritated the membranes unless you took massive doses of vitamin C simultaneously so your nose wouldn't run.

Harvey patted her neat little rump reassuringly, poured the Fetzer, passed the runny Rouge et Noir Brie and listened to eclectic scraps of conversation: "I don't care what Michael Wornum *says;* I just love his accent." . . . "est changed my whole life. I never knew before what a total shit I was." . . . "I mean, all you can finally be, *finally,* is your own person, right? I kept telling him, if he was on a different trip that was *his* problem and he was the one who had to deal with it." . . . "Sure, Marin's great, but it's a middle-class white ghetto. Why aren't they building anything decent for thirty-nine five anymore?" . . . "Hey, wow, have you had the Brie? It's practically *decadent.*"

Suffused with a happy glow because his party was really cooking, Harvey felt a sympathetic pang for Kate, her selfish insistence that he couldn't take the ficus *or* the Kentia palm notwithstanding. Was Kate also happy? Was she finding herself, too? . . .

9. Kate's turn

Kate told her friends how happy she was that she and Harvey had decided to split for a while, because it would give them a chance to get clear, and because her philosophy, like Sartre's, was that everybody was ultimately responsible for his own number.

She was even laid back, at least publicly, about Harvey's liaison with Marlene, the eighteen-year-old Safeway checker he was living with in that plastic condo in Greenbrae. If Harvey thought getting it on with some bubble-gum rocker was realizing his full human potential, well, that was his prerogative—although she *was* disappointed that he'd go that route because it was all so predictable. Every husband Kate knew took up with some little postadolescent with acne as soon as he split from his wife.

She realized it had to do with the whole macho bit in Western culture. In his pathetic way, Harvey was trying to prove something. She did, however, resent the fact that he was uptight about the support money he gave her and complained all the time about his "cash flow." It wasn't her fault, as she told Carol, if he was having a tough time keeping Marlene in Motown records and Clearasil.

Therefore, she took a hard line that last time he called her to say her check was going to be late, asked him sweetly if Marlene needed orthodontia, and threatened to call her lawyer. She needed money if she was going to put it all together and lead her own new liberated life.

In the first few heady weeks of freedom after Harvey left, Kate tried to write. She'd always thought she had a really sensitive novel in her. But when she bought a lot of yellow legal pads, sharpened some No. 2 pencils and sat down to create, nothing happened and she ended up making grocery lists. Mature self-expression apparently came only with time and serenity.

Then she thought she'd like to open a little restaurant, an intimate place featuring one really unusual ethnic entrée a night and her secret-formula curried salad dressing, for people who were seriously into food. But she didn't know where to start after she'd looked up "Restaurant Suppliers" in the yellow pages and shortly abandoned that project, too.

Maybe she'd move to Bolinas for a few months, meet some mellow West Marin types, and get back to nature; she could romp on the beach with the Afghan, and

Michael Bry would happen along and do this photo essay on her as a "woman in transition." With all that space, she and Joan could learn to relate to each other as persons, instead of "mother" and "daughter" (Kate had had it with role-playing), and they could make a little money raising organic chickens or something.

But Joan told her what she could do with Bolinas and all that chicken shit, so contingency plan number three disintegrated, too. All she had to show for it was the photogenic yellow windbreaker she'd bought herself at Battens and Boards.

The problem, of course, was that Kate couldn't really get her act together while she was worrying about how she was going to pay her guitar teacher and where her next pair of Adidas was coming from. So she kept on tying knots in plant hangers, although macramé was practically destroying her fingernails, and went off to the Marin City flea market every Saturday morning to peddle them. She had to do *something* until she found out just where her major talent actually lay.

Kate met Phil there one freezing morning when she was setting up her display in the back of the VW bus and he was arranging his stock of pre-worn-out Levi's on a blanket in front of his camper. You had to arrive there by six or so if you were going to get a good location. The fog was hanging dankly over the parking lot, and Kate was shivering. She was wearing her tap-dancing shorts from the Poppy Shoppe that day because she didn't tap-dance and had to wear them somewhere.

She went over to ask Phil if she could borrow a pair of jeans, he sold her some for fifteen dollars and a plant hanger, and she offered him a cup of Earl Grey from her Thermos bottle. It wasn't exactly wildly romantic, but the demon lover Kate had fantasized as waiting to pounce on her the moment Harvey was safely out of the way hadn't materialized. In fact, nobody had even propositioned her, except for Harvey's friend Jerry from the car pool, who had bad breath, still said "Right on," and had phoned her one night to ask her bluntly if she was "hot to trot."

So she was ready for it when Phil asked her, at the end of a slow day, if she'd like to go back to his place, drink some wine and maybe turn on. Kate felt she ought to broaden her experience. Specifically, she thought she ought to broaden it just the way Harvey had broadened his.

It turned out, though, when she parked the bus behind Phil's camper and followed him to his Sausalito houseboat, that Phil had something more exotic in mind than she did. It took her about thirty seconds once she'd made her way down the board-walk after him (stoically ignoring the floating

turds bobbing alongside) to register a collection of sinister-looking whips among the crud in his combination kitchen, head and living room. And there weren't any mule teams in Marin.

"You into pain?" Phil asked her, as he poured her a cheese glass full of Foppiano red. Kate said not exactly. Phil handed her the smeary glass and simultaneously pinched her thigh hard. "Trust me," he said. "It's a new taste thrill."

Now that Phil had taken off his shades, Kate could see that he had crazy eyes. He also had a beard like a Brillo pad and a middle-aged paunch. No use conning herself: her reality principle told her that Phil wasn't the demon lover she had in mind; he was just your ordinary sadomasochist freak. She was working up to her full anxiety quotient, wondering what she'd got herself into, when the door of the houseboat opened and in came a woman who weighed about two hundred pounds and was wearing Waffle-Stompers and a muu-muu.

The woman regarded Kate with malevolent little eyes. "My old lady," Phil said. "Don't worry. Miriam's easy; she swings either way." He pinched her again. "How about we all smoke a little dope and mellow out, okay?"

Kate bolted. She was in her bus, sweating after her full-throttle flight down the board-walk, before she remembered that the Levi's she'd bought from him were still in the back of Phil's camper. Fifteen dollars down the tube on top of everything else, she thought angrily. And what was Harvey doing while she was wearing her fingers to the bone tying those endless goddamn knots and fighting off Jack the Whipper? Was he really as happy with his teen-aged concubine as he was advertising he was?

10. Harvey's options

Harvey told everyone that living with Marlene was fantastic; but if he'd been really upfront, their relationship wasn't entirely a waterbed of roses.

Marlene was basically a beautiful human being, and you couldn't beat her for sensory gratification. But she was very young, and having an eighteen-year-old mistress, Harvey was finding, was a mixed bag.

Back when he was living with Kate, and Marlene was still only a fantasy, he hadn't flashed on how old and decrepit it would make him feel, when they bicycled together, to struggle up the grade from Sausalito on his Motobecane with Marlene already halfway across the Golden Gate Bridge on her heavy Schwinn Collegiate. He hadn't anticipated that she'd run him all over the tennis court at the Mount Tam Racquet Club and then suggest, while he was still fending off massive coronary arrest, that they jog back to the condo. And he was still reeling from her question the other night, while they were watching *Eleanor and Franklin* on TV, about whether he'd ever voted for Teddy Roosevelt.

Marlene hadn't meant to put him down. She didn't have a mean bone in her body, and Harvey sometimes suspected she didn't have any bones at all. It was just that she lacked historical perspective. Marlene's idea of ancient history was the Cuban missile crisis.

Then, too, living with Marlene reminded him inevitably of life with his daughter Joan, and Harvey had found Joan incomprehensible for years, ever since she'd turned thirteen and had started looking at him as if he were an Eisenhower Republican. Like Joan, Marlene washed her hair constantly. She went through mind-boggling quantities of Earth Born Shampoo and lemon creme rinse, and once came out of the bathroom to announce that they were out of both with an expression that suggested she was suffering from incurable bone cancer. Like Joan's, Marlene's entire range of expression was pretty much limited to "far out," "super" and "gross." And like Joan, Marlene was a raving fanatic about nutrition; she lectured Harvey endlessly about things like the body's need for zinc, and wasn't amused when he suggested amiably that they go out and chew on the Volvo bumper.

Recently, for instance, the barbecue-flavor Fritos had really hit the fan when Marlene had caught him furtively wolfing them down in the bathroom with the water running for cover. First she screamed at him that if he was going to poison himself on chemical preservatives, she "couldn't be responsible." Then she made him drink a quart of kefir to "neutralize the toxins."

Harvey had never been a junk-food junkie, but he was now driven by Marlene's organic cuisine, which ran heavily to millet, to sneaking off to the San Rafael A & W for Papaburgers. Ordering a Papaburger embarrassed him, but the alternative was a Mamaburger or a Babyburger, and while Papaburgers weren't exactly his idea of a gastronomic high, they bore some remote resemblance to meat. Marlene, shuddering with revulsion, called meat "animal flesh," and wouldn't have it anywhere on her turf.

Actually, Harvey had never been big on Kate's gourmet tripping either. The month before he left, she was taking Nancy Jue's cooking class at the Co-op and everything she served him had been "chowed." Nonetheless, it looked pretty good in retrospect. And so did Kate.

Kate had been Harvey's idea of a royal Bengal pain in the ass for the last year, while she was "coming out of the broom closet," as she put it, but the worst was behind. She had somehow reconciled shaving her legs with the Movement and no longer held Harvey personally responsible for the oppression of women down through the ages. Recently she'd even sympathized with him a little about the way he'd been "programmed" to think he was a man instead of a human being.

Furthermore, Kate didn't wig out over the occasional Frito, didn't consider his J. C. Penney's boxer shorts "gross," and didn't even laugh at him when, preparing for a weekend of backpacking, he filed most of the handle off his toothbrush. She even packed his Sominex and his Ace bandages.

On the flip side, sometimes life with Marlene was incredibly mellow. They ate leisurely brunches together at The Crossroads on Sunday mornings (Marlene knew a chick who worked there and assured Harvey that the food was absolutely free of toxins), went off to River City to catch Stoneground (predictably enough, Marlene's favorite rock band), and watched old movies like *Rebel Without a Cause* on the late, late show while they munched Marlene's inimitable toasted soybeans.

They also spent a lot of time in the waterbed, or more precisely, on it; but Harvey found Marlene's superior muscle tone a bit of a problem there, too, and what with missing a somewhat less rigorous domestic scene, the Afghan and his compost grinder—the trash compactor in the condo just didn't do it for him—he was starting to think it was time he and Kate had a good rap about redefining the parameters of their relationship.

One afternoon he called her and suggested that they could maybe get together at 464, eat a little meat and carry on a meaningful dialogue. He planned to tell Marlene that he was working late at the bank; Kate had always bought it, so why wouldn't she?

But Kate asked him nastily if Marlene was coming along and if he wouldn't rather go to Lyons, where they had children's menus. She also said she wasn't about to give up her freedom for a whole evening just because Marlene had to go out selling Girl Scout cookies or something and Harvey didn't have enough "inner resources" to entertain himself.

Harvey countered furiously that Kate was still making this really dumb mistake: she was still confusing being a liberated woman with being a nickel-plated bitch. He then asked to speak to Joan, because if Kate was going to do a number like that on him, he'd take his daughter to dinner instead. Joan used to love it when he took her to the zoo. But Joan told him he was "gross" and a dirty old man and hung up on him so hard it made his eyes water.

Bleakly, Harvey contemplated the evening ahead. *Rhoda, Phyllis,* and maybe a late-night rerun of *The Brady Bunch.* In desperation, because he really needed to relate to another grownup for a few hours, Harvey decided to call Kate's freaky friend Carol. . . .

11. A change of pace

When the news of Kate's and Harvey's separation reached Martha, the friend whose Mount Tam wedding they'd attended a few months before, it really got to her. Her gut reaction, as she told her new husband Bill, was "You gotta be kidding!"

The split, however, was for real. Several people all confirmed it, though there was some confusion about whether Harvey was living with a fourteen-year-old female mainliner or a male hairdresser.

Martha was cool about that part: different strokes and like that. But she felt really paranoid about the breakup of the marriage, because if the Holroyds couldn't make it, who could? They'd seemed so *together* together. And Martha was genuinely fond of them both, even if they were heavily into that whole suburban materialistic bag.

Reciting Rod McKuen to the Boston ferns in her Fairfax Canyon A-frame, baking whole-grain pumpernickel and reading *Jonathan Livingston Seagull* to the children (they knew it by heart but clamored for it anyway), Martha did some deep thinking about marriage. After five of them, she felt she had some insight on the subject, and one thing she had learned, while she was paying her dues, was that marriage was this dynamic process. You had to stay really in touch with yourself if you were going to relate to the other person's feelings instead of just ego-tripping.

Bill said you shouldn't judge anybody else until you'd walked a mile in his hiking boots, but Martha couldn't help wondering, nonetheless, if the Holroyds' separation wasn't one more spin-off from Watergate. Not that she thought the CIA had sent Kate obscene tape recordings or anything—she wasn't *that* paranoid—but her own last marriage had deteriorated rapidly when Nixon finally resigned. Almost immediately, she and her ex had realized that they didn't have anything else to talk about.

While life, too, was a process, and all experience was good if you took the cosmic overview, Martha knew from personal experience that failure *felt* like a bummer at the time. She knew she ought to call Kate and invite her to dinner, or at least encourage her to dump on her and get her feelings right upfront where Martha could help her work through them.

She kept procrastinating, though, because the Holroyd bit threatened her, in view of her own new permanent commitment, and she thought she'd better get clear on the whole shtick herself before she got in-

volved. After all, she and Bill were still getting inside each other's heads, a high-energy trip that didn't leave a lot of space for outside interaction.

Consequently, Martha was particularly freaked out when she learned accidentally that Harvey was now involved with Carol, Kate's friend and Martha's own.

The first time she saw them together; picking out a Camembert at The Cheese Store in Old Brown's, she didn't put it together; lots of people were into Camembert, so maybe it was no big thing. Certainly Carol was dressed to kill, in a forties dress from Foxy Lady and the platforms Martha had admired in the window of Wanda's Boutique/Footique the week before, but Carol always dressed like a Pointer Sister anyway. And they were both laid back. Harvey even invited Martha to drop by his condo on the Greenbrae canal some afternoon and feed the ducks.

The next time she encountered the two of them, at the new Saturday Night Movie series in that funky old Odd Fellows Hall on Throckmorton, Martha just figured Harvey's hairdresser lover had already seen *Payday*. If he and Carol were getting it on, wouldn't they be keeping a low profile? Anyway, it had always been Martha's impression that Harvey didn't like Carol. You didn't go to bed with someone you couldn't even *relate* to.

Finally, however, she saw Harvey and Carol practically crawling all over each other in the parking lot in front of Caruso's one Saturday afternoon. There they were, squashed together in the driver's seat of Harvey's familiar Volvo with the bumper sticker that read "I'd Rather Be Sailing."

Martha wound her way back up Scenic deeply upset. Thank God it wasn't her problem, because after all those years of unhappy marriages to psychotics, all of whose self-images were based on destroying hers, she'd earned the right to just look after Numero Uno. But she was burned at Carol. Sisterhood was powerful, for sure, but it ought to stop short, in Martha's view, of incest.

She and Bill rapped about the whole

thing in depth that night over the cioppino. It was a somewhat fragmented conversation, because Tamalpa, Martha's four-year-old from her second marriage, kept throwing clams at Bill's son Gregor from his last permanent commitment, and a lot of the time was necessarily devoted to an open discussion of sibling rivalry and the extended-family concept. Nonetheless, Bill convinced Martha that she should probably tell Kate, because if you weren't part of the solution, you were part of the problem. How could Kate deal with the realities of her particular time and space if she didn't know what they were?

Martha agreed to call Kate as soon as she'd scraped the tomato sauce out of the natural Iranian rug from Rezaian's that was the only positive carry-over from her last domestic interlude, but she wasn't very happy about the prospect. What if Kate somehow blamed her? Like subconsciously?

Fortunately, she didn't have to cope right away; the Maginnises, who lived next door and whose kids went to the same alternative nursery school as hers and Bill's, were coming over for coffee. By the time Martha got the kids to stop trying to mug each other and settled them in front of their respective easels for their regular half hour of free expression, it was time to grind the French roast for the Chemex.

Martha was looking forward to some stimulating adult conversation, since it was hard to keep your mind alive when you spent most of your life with people three feet high. While she was standing at the sink digging the play-dough out of her demitasse cups, she also had a flash that made her feel a lot more integrated about Kate, Harvey and that whole scene. If anybody could tell her whether or not she should be upfront with Kate or take part in the cover-up, it was Naomi Maginnis. Naomi, a heavy-duty intellectual, was practically Martha's guru. . . .

12. Dealing with the whole child

Kate's friend Martha and her husband Bill shared with their Fairfax next-door neighbors a total commitment to the nurturing of the whole child, so they had a lot in common even though Martha was a college dropout while Naomi Maginnis had two master's degrees from Mills, one in sociology and one in batik.

It just went to show that intellectual heavies could be beautiful in spite of all those smarts. Naomi, for instance, was a model mother. Unlike Martha herself, she never shouted at her kids, never blew her cool with them and never came on like a parent figure. Look at the way she was now persuading her youngest, John Muir Maginnis, to stop swinging on Martha's drapes.

"John-John," Naomi was saying, "I shouldn't engage in that form of activity if I were you. Your actions might be subject to misinterpretation, don't you agree?"

John-John stared at her balefully. "I don' give a shit," he said, and instead began to beat Tamalpa, Martha's four-year-old daughter, over the head with his Playskool carpenter's awl. It was just amazing the way children worked out their hostilities among themselves if you didn't interfere with their natural instincts.

Serving the coffee and her homemade whole-wheat baklava, Martha thought about the way parents in Marin raised their young. The contrast to her own oppressively regimented childhood made her feel truly optimistic about the future of humanity in the hands of Consciousness III. If, like Tamalpa and John-John, she had been permitted as a child to "act out" when she felt like it, Martha was pretty sure she wouldn't have spent all those years in psychoanalysis. Her shrink had told her that her own father, as she'd described him, was practically a casebook example of an anal retentive.

It did worry her, occasionally, that her oldest daughter, Debbie, had gone all through high school in Marin without learning to write a grammatical sentence and without knowing where Europe was. (Debbie got Europe mixed up with Eureka.) But Martha had discussed the whole thing with Debbie's counselor on more than one occasion and had found him terrifically *simpático;* he'd pointed out to her that the written word was on its way out, that what was most important was that Debbie learn to function in the here/now, and that Martha must want her daughter to be happy.

Martha hadn't heard from Debbie since she ran off to Zihuatanejo with a dirt-bike racer, so she didn't know whether Debbie was really, *really* happy or not. But she was glad she had a chance to parent all over again with Tamalpa, Gregor and Che.

She sat down beside Naomi on her new natural linen sofa from McDermott's (Martha was getting back to natural fibers and earthy colors, because your environment was terrifically important to your inner serenity), and started to ask her, as she'd planned to do earlier, about whether or not she should tell Kate about Harvey's new liaison. Naomi was the person to give her the straight dope, because while she didn't know either of the Holroyds, she not only belonged to Mensa but was fantastic at conceptualizing.

But John-John sort of blew it by picking up his father's coffee cup and dumping the scalding French roast methodically down his pant leg, which caused Jason, who usually didn't overreact like that, to scream. So they had to drop everything else for the moment and explain the pleasure/pain principle to him, and Martha had to get a sponge and mop up the coffee from the natural linen, a little nostalgic for the old Naugahyde sofa it had replaced. Of course she wouldn't have plastic in her house anymore, because it was so *synthetic*, but sometimes she missed it.

Jason was superintelligent, too, however (he had a Ph.D. in Medieval Studies from Cornell and was currently teaching night classes in bonehead English at the College of Marin), so he naturally dealt with John-John calmly once he stopped writhing. "John," he said, "I can only surmise that your impulsive gesture, in pouring hot coffee on your father, was the result of some instinctual aversion to the use of stimulants—an admirable course of action in the abstract but a painful one in actuality. I feel we should discuss the question of how one chooses the form of protest he employs as a vehicle for his convictions. It's difficult to entertain an honest difference of opinion on the rational level when one is suffering from third-degree burns, can you understand that?"

John-John gave him the finger, snatched Martha's baklava off her plate and began to pull Gregor's hair. Martha thought it really spoke volumes for the Maginnises that he was so uninhibited.

Finally, although the intrusion of the children continued to be a problem throughout the evening, Martha and Bill brought the conversation around to what Martha should do about Kate. Was it more authentic to tell her that Harvey was getting it on with Carol, whom Kate thought of as her best friend, or just to cop out?

Naomi resolved the issue definitively once she'd gently restrained Gregor from kicking her repeatedly in the calf of her Danskin leotard. "Look, Martha," she said, "while my opinion is necessarily 'off the wall,' as you'd put it, I should think that your dilemma, as you've articulated it, has wider implications.... John-John, Mummy finds it unpleasant to be poked in the eye like that.... I myself feel that absolute honesty must always take precedence, in an enlightened community, over crasser, more pragmatic considerations. Otherwise we simply recreate the hypocrisy of our times, with all its disastrous and perhaps irrevocable consequences.

"I, for one, would want to know if Jason were betraying me in that particularly squalid fashion ..." Naomi paused meaningfully ... "so I could *kill* the son-of-a-bitch."

Martha was just zapped. Naomi *always* got right down to the nitty-gritty. "Wow," she said, "you're right. You're right, you know? Really." As soon as the Maginnises went home, if they ever did, she was determined to call Kate, painful duty though it was, and give her the word. ...

13. Kate wonders what it all means

It sent Kate really into the pits when she learned from her "friend" Martha, who seemed to get off on laying bad trips on people, that Harvey was now getting it on with Carol. Her first impulse was to call him and let him know that she thought he'd schizzed out completely. First he'd gone in for child-molesting—that chick he was living with in Greenbrae was practically a *baby*—and now he'd taken up with a woman he'd always said he thought was a total flake. What, exactly, was Harvey's *problem?*

She kept her cool, since Harvey and his hangups were no longer her problem. He'd made his waterbed and he could lie in it, although she couldn't help wishing that both he and his Innerspace would spring a leak.

What boggled her, though, was why her uptight husband, who'd always struck most of the women she knew as a superstraight with a button-down, banker's mind, was suddenly a sex symbol to women who formerly wouldn't even tell him what time it was. The answer, of course, was that

Harvey was simply a single male in a sellers' market. It nonetheless surprised Kate that Carol would have anything to do with him. What had happened to *her* ex, the graphics artist who'd embellished Carol's converted van with "U.S. Male" in Art Deco lettering?

Carol had been having problems with the dude when she joined their consciousness-raising group, having got tired, she explained, of being knocked unconscious. But she'd been optimistic that she and Roberto could "work through it." Roberto was in heavy therapy and was starting to have some insights about himself. Carol had told the group how he'd realized recently that the reason he knocked her around like that was that he was really terrifically *vulnerable* himself.

Kate supposed that for Carol, Harvey represented some sort of progress. At least he wasn't addicted to a combination of cocaine and Boone's Farm Apple. And certainly she herself had never gone along with that "marriage as possession" bit. The news was still a downer, though, because if you couldn't trust your own sisters, how could you count on a really open, caring relationship with anybody?

Meanwhile, her own new life remained largely unsatisfying. For one thing, her daughter Joan was becoming more and more difficult. Kate had thought that with

Harvey out of the tract house and all those bad vibes no longer coming down, she and Joan could develop a really terrific woman-to-woman relationship. This morning, however, they'd had a really heavy confrontation when Joan had started off for Tam High in her halter top from The Wildflower, her platform wedgies, and not much else. "What do you *want* me to wear?" she'd screamed, when Kate attempted to interfere. "*Clothes?*"

Then, too, her own attempts to extend her parameters and open herself up to experience hadn't amounted to much these last few months. First she'd had that cliff-hanger with Phil, the archfreak from the flea market, whose ads for "open-minded fems. with whip fantasies" she'd since recognized in the *Berkeley Barb*.

Next she'd met Frank, while she was taking a break at Fred's one afternoon in between her half-hearted attempts to get a job and start doing meaningful work. Frank had shared his table, given her some honey out of his private stash for her iced tea and told her, two minutes after he'd met her, his whole life story, practically. Right away they'd flashed on how much their trips were alike, because he, too, had just split from a paranoid psychotic and was presently giving first priority to getting his head together.

Kate had taken his telephone number when he left Fred's, absent-mindedly leaving her to pay for his tuna salad special, and after a few tics and twitches, had finally called and asked him to dinner. Now that traditional sex-role stereotypes had crumbled, women no longer had to be passive.

That was that—*finito*. Frank told her that he'd have to let her know, then called back to say both the *I Ching* and his dreambook indicated strongly that if he saw her anytime in the next three months, their relationship would suffer. Kate made a note in her Sierra Club datebook to check with him again in May, but she wasn't optimistic.

Her job search having fizzled out, too, since what she had to offer wasn't what she could do, exactly, but what she *was* and there was so much discrimination against women in the marketplace, Kate had a lot of time on her hands. Not that it was *wasted*, because she still had her yoga classes, at this incredible private home in Ross that had won an award from *Sunset* last year, her macramé and her terrifically creative inner life. And she was taking conversational French at the College of Marin on Wednesday nights just in case she ever decided to be a day student and really tune in to the whole "reentry woman" head-set.

But it wasn't the total fulfillment she had in mind, any of it, and living alone was really forcing her to confront some painful aspects of the reality principle. For one thing, she realized she didn't actually, truly,

ultimately have any real friends, anybody who knew where she was coming from and where she was at. Not only had her women friends, who should have been a positive-reinforcement support group, not introduced her to any fabulous new men she could really dig on; they never even invited her to those intimate little dinner parties that were the Real Marin anymore.

How Kate missed them: the rap sessions about politics, the gourmet goodies, the wine tripping ... the whole vital, eclectic gestalt. Sitting on the deck of the Mill Valley Library the afternoon after Martha's call, looking out over the redwoods and trying to transcend the Harvey/Carol thing, Kate decided that if her women friends were threatened by her new status as a foxy, available female in a sexually emancipated society, she herself would have to seize the initiative. She'd just have to be aggressive—in the *positive* sense.

The Mill Valley Library, however, wasn't the place to put it together. Kate had sort of drifted into it because she thought it would be mellow in the middle of the afternoon and a good place to meditate. And at first it seemed okay, once she got through the mass of snarling German shepherds perennially fighting on the front porch while they waited for their owners to finish reading *The Nation* and the *Evergreen Review* in the periodical section.

But inside, it looked like something out of *The Emigrants,* with all those pioneer types coming to America in steerage. Bodies draped all over the Espenet couches. Toddlers wailing forlornly in the stacks. Grade school rockers plugged into all the earphones and stomping on the wall-to-wall carpet as they freaked out on Led Zeppelin. Women with bare midriffs and string shopping bags rummaging through the McNaughtons and discussing Anaïs Nin. The noise level was close to the pollution level, and Kate had a low pain threshold.

She decided to plan her own marvelous Marin party at home, collected her Afghan from the dog pack and split. First, however, in the interests of getting clear, she was going to have it out with Harvey about Carol. . . .

14. Emergency at Marin General

The night Kate called Harvey, practically in hysterics, to ask how he could *do* that to her—getting it on with her best friend like that—Harvey didn't have any answers. He couldn't figure out how the whole scene with Carol had got off the launching pad, either, and what was even stickier, he couldn't get a handle on how his new life as an emancipated man in Marin had become so incredibly complicated in general.

What he had had in mind, when he split from the tract house and all it stood for, was "the simple life." Now Kate, her voice rising and falling like a fire siren, was screaming at him that while she didn't give a damn, of course, "only sickies went in for child-molesting." What did he do, she demanded shrilly, when Marlene was "off playing with her little friends? Hang around school playgrounds?"

And "what was he going to do for an encore" now that he'd taken up with Carol, a card-carrying freak who usually had nothing to do with straights like Harvey? Get one ear pierced? Dye his hair green? Maybe he could take lessons at Family Light and learn to play backup on electric sitar. Kate was sure that with her connections, Carol could get him a job watering plants for Bill Graham until he really got his act together. . . .

She went on and on, while Harvey produced a series of carefully modulated grunts in response, keeping a wary eye on Marlene. Marlene was pretending not to listen, but had stopped singing along with the sound track from *Nashville* and was keeping a watchful eye upon him.

Meanwhile, Carol was waiting for him across the freeway at the bar in Victoria Station. Victoria Station's remodeled railway cars reminded Harvey uncomfortably of his exhausting evening commute between the condo and Marlene, "U.S. Male" and Carol, and Marin and the Wells Fargo Bank, where his secretary, Ms. Murphy, was currently making his daylight hours stressful as well.

Now that he was more or less single, Ms. Murphy had suddenly decided Harvey was "a total turn-on," a switch because she'd previously been the one piling up the sandbags against his own spring offensive. Had things been different on the home front, he would have swung with this development; but now the bank was his only refuge. He didn't appreciate Ms. Murphy's energetic attempts to talk him into noon-hour matinees when she should have been trying to get her carbon paper in with the shiny side down.

Harvey found his new image mind-boggling. Had the word come down that he'd inherited a bundle? Been to Switzerland for goat-gland transplants? Knew where to get squash-blossom necklaces wholesale?

Or, as Carol assured him, had he really been smoldering with "this fantastic repressed sexuality" all along during those domestic years when the high point of his week was coming home to find the latest *Newsweek* on the coffee table? It didn't seem likely. For one thing, Marlene was obviously trying to tell him something; she'd recently stepped up his daily vitamin E intake to the overdose level. For another, he'd been driven by his own fears of inadequacy to sneaking into the Star Herb Company on Miller for herbal aphrodisiacs "for a friend."

None of them seemed to do much good in the final analysis, and if anything tasted worse than ginseng, Harvey had yet to discover it. Ginseng tea tasted like antifreeze. Furthermore, he was pretty sure he was allergic to the stuff, and allergies were nothing to fool around with. Kate had once told him about a woman friend of hers who had practically *died* after she went to a "sensory awareness" session, allowed herself to be communally massaged, and later discovered she was allergic to body lotion.

Trying to think about other things as Kate's voice continued to pound his ear,

Harvey had a terrifying flash: what if he *wasn't* allergic to ginseng and that irritating little rash of his couldn't be attributed to his Peter Pan bicycle shorts either? A doctor he knew from the annual Tinsley Island regatta, Marin's version of those tony Bohemian Club drink-ins, had recently told him about a new strain of veneral disease—"LGV"—that was sweeping Marin. The doctor had jocularly called it "brothel sprouts."

Harvey hung up abruptly on Kate, left a bewildered Marlene in the middle of the thirty-second chorus of "It Don't Worry Me," and bolted for the emergency room of Marin General. He knew he was being paranoid and that sordid social diseases didn't strike healthy, middle-class escrow officers, but he couldn't help freaking out anyway. Carol's van had a lot of mileage on it, and so, he suspected, did Carol.

At ten o'clock on a Saturday night, the emergency room was getting more of the action than Positively Fourth Street. Harvey had a hard time convincing the receptionist, to whom he whispered his complaint, that a slight rash was any big deal and just about fled when she asked to have a look at it. Eventually, however, he was allowed to sign in, a process that involved a lot of paper work about his medical insurance, his financial status and his executor. Declining an offer to sit in on a bridge game and another to join a euphoric bunch smoking dope in the corner (they were passing the time with a friend who had a broken arm but was feeling no pain), he waited grimly for his turn.

It came about two in the morning, after Harvey had observed a gurney rolling by with a hang glider who had hung too loose, the doper falling off his chair and possibly breaking the other arm, and a weary doctor chewing out the fifth woman that night who'd come in with "French-bread thumb." It seemed that half the women in Marin gave Saturday-night dinner parties, drank too much with the hors d'oeuvres and then sliced their thumbs instead of the French bread when they finally stumbled into the kitchen to serve the beef Burgundy.

The doctor was having a lot of trouble sewing up all those thumbs because his own thumb was bandaged; he'd cut it, he guiltily admitted, shucking oysters late at night at Sea Ranch the weekend before.

The steady procession into the examining room reminded Harvey of the final scene of *The Seventh Seal*, but he himself was finally permitted to dance across the horizon. What happened next was a particularly humiliating version of a "good news/bad news" joke. Harvey was given a clean bill of health and told to lay off ginseng. He was also informed by the doctor on duty, who of course just *had* to be a tennis friend, that he and his wife were going to a dinner party at Kate's next weekend.

The friend promised to honor the sacred doctor-patient relationship, but what with one thing and another, Harvey was beginning to wonder just how long he could survive the joys of being a liberated Marin male. . . .

15. A dinner to remember

At two in the morning, when the Wilsons, the Gallaghers and the Steins finally finished off the last of the Courvoisier and left, each of them assuring her that dinner had been "fabulous," Kate surveyed the rubble in her tract house kitchen in a happy glow of accomplishment. All that work had paid off; she was back in the mainstream again, her credentials as a Marin hostess reestablished.

And she'd pulled off her party without Harvey, who'd always driven her up the wall, on similar occasions in the past, worrying about whether she hadn't served the Gallaghers *ris de veau* the last time they were there, whether or not Petrini's pâté was overexposed as an hors d'oeuvre, and whether the people she'd invited would really relate to each other or have to fake it.

One of Harvey's uptight ideas, for instance, was that you never invited a doctor and a lawyer to the same party because they'd spend the evening hassling each other about the malpractice insurance crisis. Scratch *that* little bit of folk wisdom. Frank Gallagher was a surgeon, Tony Wilson an attorney; and not only had they never even *mentioned* malpractice insurance tonight, they'd scarcely even made eye contact.

As for Petrini's pâté, Angela Stein had greeted its entrance, over the perfect Manhattans, with glad little cries. She said she loved Petrini's pâté and *nobody* ever served it anymore.

Of course there *were* minor hassles over the evening. A dinner party wasn't a well-oiled machine or something. It was sort of more like a compost heap, where you just put everything in and turned the hose on it and hoped it would turn into mulch. But you couldn't expect pyracantha trimmings and potato peels to break down into organic matter at exactly the same rate, and sometimes you got a lot of fruit flies. . . .

Scraping congealed Bordelaise off her Heath ware plates, Kate abandoned the comparison. Her party hadn't *decomposed*, though she had been kind of freaked out when it developed that Marsha Wilson had become a lacto-vegetarian since Kate had last seen her. Marsha had accordingly preempted the entire wilted-spinach salad. And Kate thought it insensitive of Ginger Gallagher to hold forth, over the beef Wellington, about *Diet for a Small Planet* and how selfish it was for middle-class WASPs to eat meat instead of soybeans and screw up the entire protein chain.

Ginger's remark burned Kate especially

since she hadn't been invited to dinner parties herself lately, because friends apparently felt she needed space, and she'd had some heavy anxieties about the menu anyway. She wasn't sure what was really *au courant* right now, and the Marin dinner-party number went through like *cycles.*

Ten years ago, when she and Harvey had first moved to Mill Valley and started making the scene, it was easy; if you had people to dinner, you just cooked yourself blind. Kate and all her women friends competed with each other to serve the first really authentic couscous or the first Mongolian hot-pot, complete with those little mesh dippers from Cost Plus you passed around so each guest could fish out his own individual bits of bok choy.

At that point in time, food was *big,* because everybody else, too, had just discovered it, after migrating to the Bay Area from Indiana or some godforsaken place, and gourmet tripping was the name of the game. You could just wipe everybody *out* by stuffing your own grape leaves, making your own phyllo dough or pickling your own pickled squid.

Then came phase two, when everybody got tired of pickled squid and stuffed grape leaves and decided food was *fuel* and that placing all that emphasis on it was "decadent." During phase two, Kate planted her Mongolian hot-pot with Swedish ivy. She

no longer cooked three-day Julia Child spectaculars but instead called people at five o'clock, just off the wall, to ask them to drop around and take pot luck with "the family" if they didn't have anything else going. She promised not to fuss and said she'd "just dump another quart of water into the lentil soup."

For the last three weeks she'd worried about whether phase two was still in effect or not. Had "getting back to the basics" also become decadent, while she was still too hung up in her own scene with Harvey to pick up on it? She seemed to remember her ex-friend Martha's recently describing some real losers as "the kind of people who still serve California wines."

Kate started the first load of Heath ware in

the Kitchenaid, started hand-washing her tulip glasses, and consigned the last of the beef Wellington to the Afghan (nothing was worse than puff paste on the second day). There wasn't much left, so she must have been doing something right, and certainly the high-energy rap they'd had over the evening reinforced her sense of really having made it dinner-partywise.

For starters, she and Ginger Gallagher had had this great conversation about choosing a gynecologist who could really relate to women even if he wasn't one. Ginger had said the critical thing was whether or not he had *Our Bodies, Ourselves* in the waiting room instead of *Penthouse* or *Field and Stream*.

Frank Gallagher and Sam Stein had talked for *hours* about the energy crisis and how they were going to build solar heating units for their swimming pools. Frank said that if everybody else did the same thing, we wouldn't have to worry about the Arab oil cartel anymore.

And over the bisque, Marsha Wilson, who sold real estate, had filled them all in on the housing market, which made Kate feel a lot more *secure* about her own socioeconomic status. Marsha said Kate had a fortune right here "under the floorboards," and that even with those crummy bathrooms, she could get Kate fifty-nine five for the place tomorrow—and she was "talking dollars."

They'd also talked about environmental impact reports. Sam Stein, an urban planner, had said you practically had to have one to bear children these days. They'd traded ways of keeping the deer from eating your entire winter-vegetable garden and had been really zonked when Tony Wilson said the only thing that really worked was panther urine. They'd rapped about saunas vs. Japanese hot tubs, whether anybody really *needed* quadraphonic stereo, whether it was sexist to vote for Barbara Boxer for supervisor. . . . Looking back on it all, Kate realized that there were all these·terrifically intelligent, vital people in Marin who had practically *Renaissance* minds.

Kate's only frustration, as she turned out the lights at last and started down the hall to crash, was that she still felt high on the whole scene and wished she had someone to rap about it with. But Harvey wasn't around, thank God, and Joan had taken off for a weekend in Mendocino or someplace. She'd been pretty vague on the whole subject, but Kate had let her go because she didn't want to come on like an authority figure.

Now that she had time to think about it, though, Kate *was* a little concerned. Who the hell did Joan know in Mendocino?

16. Joan joins the Moonies

"Sam," Angela Stein said to her husband when she finally pried loose from the phone, "are you *ready* for this? Joannie Holroyd's joined the Moonies. She's living on broccoli or something in this commune up in Booneville and she says she isn't coming home. She just called Kate and laid this trip on her about how she'd found God."

"They already have a dog," Sam said. He wished Angela wouldn't rap at him in the middle of *Mary Hartman, Mary Hartman,* which he always told people was the only thing he ever watched on the tube except for KQED.

"No—God," Angela said. "You know, like religion? Listen, Kate's practically coming unglued. She just accepted this collect call, and Joan said she was really, *really* happy, and she wanted Kate to be happy for her, and she was staying up there. With her *real* family."

"Jesus!" Sam said. "I mean, poor old Kate. What's she going to do about it?"

"Well, I mean, she hasn't gotten that far," Angela said. "She's practically out of her mind. Like, she isn't even tracking . . . she keeps coming on about how Joan hates broccoli. She's trying to reach Harvey, though; that's why she called us. He isn't at the condo. She wants to know if you might know where he is, from the commute bus or something."

Sam was watching Mary Hartman's neighbor drowning in a bowl of chicken soup. He thought the joke was in crummy taste.

"Ethnic stereotyping," he said. "You ever see anybody drown in a bowl of chicken soup?"

Angela snapped off the TV. "Sam," she demanded, "will you get your act together and go look for Harvey? Like, this is a *crisis*. Do you want Joannie Holroyd peddling carnations on Bridgeway?"

Sam sighed. "I just want to see the rest of *Mary Hartman*," he said. "How should I know where Harvey is? So we ride the same commute bus. We don't exactly *confide* in each other. I mean, all I know about his scene right now is that he gets it on with a lot of women and hangs out in a lot of bars. Do you have any idea how many goddamn bars there are in Marin?"

"Will you get off God and go look for Harvey?" Angela snapped. "Listen, Kate *needs* us, okay?"

"Why don't you call her back and just ask her over to dinner or something sometime?"

"Sam, either you look for Harvey or you don't come back," Angela told him, one word at a time.

Sam wondered why women could never get behind logic. He also wondered, as he backed reluctantly out of his Ross driveway, what the hell had got into Joannie Holroyd? What had got into their own Debbie a few years ago? What had got into Marin adolescents? Didn't they all feed them, listen to them, enroll them in Mogul Ski Club? Straighten their teeth? Buy them stereos, wet suits and sailing lessons? Stay out of their sex lives and look the other way when they found their stashes?

And look what came down. Debbie had straightened out, finally, but not until they'd bailed her out of a Mexican jail, dragged her away from the Haight twice and spent one entire summer looking for her up and down the Mendocino coast before they finally found her living with some turkey in a yurt.

Frank Gallagher had complained at Kate's dinner party the other night that their oldest son, a biofeedback freak, was now one big Alpha wave. And the Wilsons, Kate's other guests, were also having heavy problems: their Nancy, who was eighteen, hadn't been heard from since she dropped out of some fancy foreign exchange program because the Sorbonne "didn't have a crisis center."

Sam thought it had something to do with the turmoil of the sixties; hadn't somebody written a book about it? In the meantime, he wished Angela hadn't got *involved*. Assuming he could find Harvey—no piece

of cake—how was he going to convince him that he should go back to the domestic ramble? From what Harvey had told him about the way he was living now, the alternative was probably an orgy. Sam knew which way he'd jump given the same options.

Harvey wasn't at Sweetwater, Zack's or the *no name*. Sam finally found him, though, wrapped around a solitary Cutty-over at the bar in the Blue Rock Inn. His tales about fighting off women only by a combination of karate and aikido notwithstanding, Harvey was alone and looked as if he were in the pits. Sam hated to do it, but Johnny Carson was practically *over*, so he just laid it on him: "Harv," he said, "you gotta go home, you know?"

Harvey stared at him.

"Joan's joined the Moonies," Sam went on. "She says she's found God."

"We already have a dog," Harvey said.

"No, man—*God*. Kate's freaking out. Joan's up in Booneville living on broccoli or something."

This time it registered. To Sam's surprise, Harvey lit up in a wide smile. "For *real?*" he asked. "You mean Kate wants me to go home? To my *house?*"

"Listen," Sam said, "what's this total shuck you've been laying on me about Maureen or whatever her name is, and Carol, and the whole bit? You *want* to go home?"

"Later," Harvey mumbled. He was already digging in his pocket for his car keys. "Listen, Sam, go by the condo for me, okay? Tell Marlene what's going down. Tell her how I've got to, like, take responsibility, you know?"

"I hear you," Sam said gloomily. No *Mary Hartman,* no Johnny Carson, and now this. Angela and her flaky "extended family concept."

He couldn't help being sort of curious about Harvey's new old lady, however. Wasn't she supposed to be fourteen or something and hooked on poppers?

Sam finished Harvey's Cutty-over, made his way out of the Blue Rock, and headed for South Eliseo. He wondered if he should call Angela and give her the word, but decided it wasn't worth it because he wouldn't be at Harvey's place for long. And anyway, Angela might be paranoid about his going to see Marlene, although Sam always agreed with her that Harvey's single-swinger number was just terrifically *immature*.

"Oh, wow," Marlene cried, when she opened the door at Harvey's place and found Sam standing there. "I thought you were Harvey and he forgot his key. Listen, something terrible's happened, right? I was just doing my horoscope, and I *flashed* on it. . . ."

Sam looked at Marlene in her halter top and her Peaches and Cream hip-huggers. He didn't know about the poppers, but she wasn't fourteen, *really*. "Look," he said soothingly, "stay cool. It's no big thing, okay?" Marlene looked as if she were going to cry. "I mean, maybe I should just kind of come in for a minute and we should talk about this. . . ."

17. Reordering the priorities

Their first priority, Kate and Harvey agreed, was to work through their conflicts, stop laying bad trips on each other, and restructure their marriage. It was a heavy number, for sure; but they could do it. For one thing, they really wanted to get it together again; and for another, living in Marin, they were part of this whole dynamic: everybody they knew was into the same process of agonizing reappraisal.

Look at Martha and Bill, for example. Not only had they agreed on an open marriage, they'd even worked out a contract before they made a permanent commitment. Kate hadn't actually seen this document, but Martha had told her how incredibly liberating it was because it spelled out *exactly* what she and Bill could expect from each other.

Bill agreed to take the garbage out three days a week. No hassles—Martha could count on it. She, for her part, had taken responsibility for Bill's laundry as well as her own and the kids', although she had insisted on a rider spelling out her right to send his shirts to Meader's. It might seem nit-picking to somebody else, she knew, but Martha couldn't get behind ironing boards, and this way, it was right there in writing.

Everything else important was spelled out ahead of the actual ceremony as well: conjugal rights, automobile maintenance, entertaining (Bill signed on to make all the salads for company dinners no matter what and to make the whole dinner when he invited *his* friends), even time off for good behavior. . . . A subclause permitted Martha to ski at Tahoe one week every winter, in January *or* February, depending on snow conditions, while Bill took over the laundry and the kids. She reciprocated by allowing Bill to go backpacking in the Sierras for ten days every summer, although due to some ambiguity in the wording of the contract, they disagreed about whether or not she should just let the garbage pile up while he was gone.

Kate thought it all sounded enlightened, because the big hangup about marriage was that people expected all these unrealistic things from their partners, like cradle-to-grave security or something. Harvey hadn't been home for a week before he asked her to take his tennis racket in to be restrung, reminded her that he didn't like Roquefort dressing, and pointed out to her that the Afghan was shedding all over his Faded Glory jacket and needed brushing.

Kate told him firmly that she wasn't going

to get into that whole "traditional wife" bit again. Hadn't he heard that Lincoln freed the slaves? Couldn't he brush the goddamn dog himself, or at least *half* the dog?

At first she thought they were going to fall into the same old syndrome that had caused them to split in the first place, because Harvey's gut reaction was to come on at her like Genghis Khan. But he finally mellowed out and agreed that Roquefort dressing was no big thing and that she, too, had a right to express her needs. The really important thing was that they come to terms about their basic lifestyle.

Kate filled Ginger in on the whole scene when she met her in the Co-op health-food store one afternoon. "It's all been good, experiencewise," she said. "I mean, we really flipped out when Joannie pulled that whole Moonie number, but it came out okay after we got her deprogrammed. I think she just needed space, you know? I think she just ran away like that because Harvey split and she had this Oedipus complex or something."

"Yeah, really," Ginger said.

"So now what we're doing is we're trying to redefine the whole family concept, because families are just terrifically heavy . . . I mean, living with other people and trying to keep your own self-concept intact. It's a problem."

"I hear you," Ginger said, sighing. "Really, I hear you."

"Anyway, all this stuff we've been through, we're all so much more in touch. We just sit around for hours and rap about our feelings, and it's just beautiful, because it's not like a family at all; it's like friends or something. It's this *flow*, you know?"

"I love it . . . I *love* it," Ginger said. "Hey, listen, have you heard about the Steins? Speaking of process?"

"No, what?"

"Sam's split. Isn't that *incredible*? I don't know what happened exactly, but he moved out on Angela. He's living with some young chick out in Lagunitas, and Angela doesn't even know exactly where. She says he hasn't even been back to get his Lhasa apso, and the last time she saw him, like going by on the freeway or something, he had this little gold ring in his ear. It just blew her away."

Kate was out in the parking lot with her Pavel's Russian yogurt before she flashed on it. . . . Marlene! Sam Stein was living with Harvey's ex, she knew it. And it was all her fault, because she was the one who had asked Sam to get involved when Joan ran away and she couldn't cope.

She felt just *terrible*. Despite the fact that she and Harvey hadn't finalized the parameters of their own interface, mainly because they still didn't agree on just how open an open marriage ought to be, they were just terrifically stable right now. Surely they couldn't just watch the Steins go through that whole separation bag and not attempt to help. Not after they'd *been* there.

When she tried to call Harvey at the bank, though, Ms. Murphy, his secretary, was terribly defensive, for some reason. "He's on another line," she said coldly. "Shall I put you on Muzak?" Then she left Kate listening to piped-in Mantovani for five minutes.

Kate gave up and called Angela Stein, but as soon as she identified herself, Angela hung up. Of course Angela was being childish, like regressing, but Kate still felt the need to hang in there and help the Steins get clear. The thing was, what could she actually *do*?

It came to her while she was starting mung beans in her sprouter: *somebody* ought to take on that promiscuous little lightweight who had seduced Harvey and was now getting it on with Sam, and Kate was the one to do it. Between her assertiveness training and her new physical fitness regime at Bob Fuller's, she was practically in shape to fight Muhammad Ali, and furthermore, she was pretty sure she knew how to track Marlene to her Lagunitas lair. . . .

18. What to wear in Woodacre

Kate liked to think that she was one of those people who could relate to practically anybody, even if their trips were entirely different. So she kept in touch, over the years, with types like her friend Rita, who had *actually* been in her high school graduating class twenty years ago in Spokane, when they were both on the Pep Squad, for God's sake, but had gone through some heavy changes since, just as Kate herself had.

Now Rita lived out in Woodacre with her old man, some other congenial freaks and a kiln. Deeply involved in the human-potential movement, she had like *mutated* over the years through Gurdjieff, Silva Mind Control, actualism, analytical tracking, parapsychology, Human Life Styling, postural integration, the Fischer-Hoffman Process, hatha and raja yoga, integral massage, orgonomy, palmistry, Neo-Reichian bodywork and Feldenkrais functional integration. Currently she was commuting to Berkeley twice a week for "polarity balancing manipulation," which, she reported through her annual mimeographed Christmas letter, produces "good thinking."

Kate found Rita's metamorphosis fascinating, because among other things, it went to show how far they'd all come from Spokane. To think she herself had grown up *programmed* like that, just taking it for granted that "success" meant a house in the suburbs, two cars and an FHA mortgage. True, she *had* a house in the suburbs, et cetera, et cetera, et cetera, but she would have been the first to insist that none of this stuff really *meant* anything. What did matter was being true to yourself, getting centered, and realizing, as another friend had so eloquently put it recently when she and Kate were rapping about self-realization, that "life was a part of existence."

That was why Kate was so anxious to reach out to Sam Stein, who was now living with the same spacy little chick who had helped Harvey avoid confronting reality for a while, and convince him that he had to get back in touch with himself and his real values. You couldn't just drop out and watch somebody else go through the same heavy number you'd been through without loving and *caring*, which was what being fully human was all about.

Rita was pleased when Kate phoned to say she needed her, and invited her out to Woodacre for "lunch or whatever's right." She said she needed a good rap, too, and it was cosmic of Kate to flash on it like that. "I mean, I've just had this letter from my *mother*, you know?" she said. "And she's, like, threatening to come down for a visit or something. I got a 'loving divorce' from my parents months ago, when I was doing Fischer-Hoffman, and I'm just not into that whole 'biological parent' bag anymore. But we can't even communicate because she practically gets *hysterical* when I try to explain it to her on the phone, and now she's flying down here with a suitcase full of chicken soup or something. I mean, I can't deal with it."

Getting dressed to go to Rita's gave Kate some trouble, because now that clothes were supposed to reflect the Inner You, getting dressed was always a problem. You couldn't just throw on clothes as if you were trying to keep warm. After some soul-searching, she decided on going Moroccan and put on her I. Magnin herdsman's caftan and her rope-tied headband. The look wasn't complete, but Harvey had been terrifically negative when she mentioned wanting to get her nose pierced, so she had to settle for her Beadazzled earrings instead. Kate loved these anyway, although they were so long they practically made her lobes hang down around her elbows.

Ready at last, she got into her bus and followed Rita's complicated directions to her Woodacre pad, a large, sprawling redwood house that had once been somebody's summer home. "Marin Establishment," as

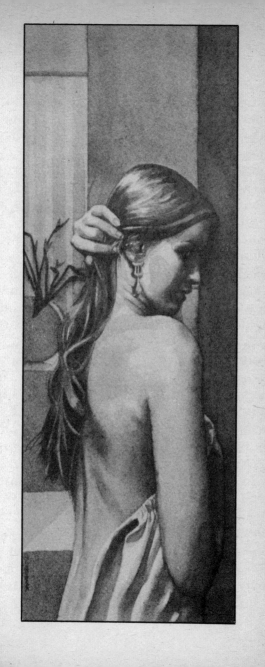

Rita put it, but practically unrecognizable after a total conceptual transformation: tie-dyed wall hangings, *real* Orientals with real moth holes in them, and Rita's incredible collection of "exotics." Rita had plants Kate had never heard of, and Kate felt momentarily abashed about her own prole Piggybacks and Creeping Charlies.

Rita herself, though, was still the same, fully actualized self. She just had this beautiful talent for creating a whole environment. "Listen," she said, "you sounded really strung out on the phone. You want to take your clothes off and really relax? I mean, *mi casa es su casa,* okay?"

Kate wasn't about to take off her clothes after she'd gone to all that trouble putting them on. She also refused Rita's offer of hash because she still had this puritanical *thing* about driving and doping. And it turned out Rita couldn't make her a salad lunch after all, because somebody had ripped off her butter lettuce, one of the hazards of living with a bunch of other vegetarians who weren't heavily into private property.

So they finally decided to sit out on the deck and just free-associate. Rita told Kate about how uptight she was about her mother's coming because it brought back Spokane and that whole head-set. "I mean, she makes *casseroles,*" Rita said. "She puts concentric circles of green pepper and pimiento on top. And she's very big on Jell-O with fruit cocktail in it, remember? And she says things like 'Undies worn twice are not very nice.' I'm freaking out just thinking about it."

Kate told her how she could dig on it and how she and Rita shared this common cultural heritage; it was just a mind-blower that they'd all *survived*. "Listen," she said, "we're very insulated, like, you know, in the Bay Area, right? I mean, we forget there are all those weird people like your mother out there. *My* mother wears Enna Jetticks, and Shelton Strollers, and Playtex Living Girdles. And *slips*. I know where you're coming from. . . ."

Finally she brought the conversation around to Marlene. Kate figured if anybody was really tuned into the whole Woodacre-Lagunitas *scene*, it was Rita. "I've got to find her," she said, "because she's incredibly destructive. She's walking bad karma. You must have seen her if she's really living out here, because she wears majorette boots."

"No way," Rita said, after a stunned silent moment. "*Nobody* in Lagunitas wears majorette boots. Funk, *sí;* bad taste, *no.*"

She promised, however, to look around and to let Kate know if she heard anything, then helped her hack a path through the woods and back to the bus, where they parted with mutual assurances of love.

"How's Harvey, anyway?" she asked, as she waved Kate off. "He still wear his Key Club pin?"

"No, *really*," Kate called back, "he's a whole new human being. You'd hardly recognize him. . . ."

19. Harvey takes responsibility

Standing in the checkout line at Goodman's one Sunday morning, Harvey found himself brooding about Life. Not that he did the heavy-duty abstract thinking in the family; that was Kate's department. But it had been a rough weekend and it wasn't over yet.

For one thing, he would rather have been doing something other than trying not to drop a fifty-pound sack of peat moss on his Adidas. For another, he and Kate were going to a wine-tasting party this afternoon, and even though Harvey was into wine himself, he hated standing around trying to think of variations on "yeasty," "fruity," "stemmy," "chewy," "corky," "acidulous," etc. If you took the long view, as Kate was always telling him to do about everything, what the hell difference did it make? Wine was just so many sour grapes anyway.

In the long view, too, what difference did the peat moss make? If life was a cabaret, why was Harvey spending half of his again standing in line at Goodman's? He was already working himself into a funk before Jerry from the car pool turned up in line be-

hind him, and from then on, it was all
downhill.

"Listen, Harv," Jerry said, "what's *with*
you? I mean, you look like you're in a funk
or something."

"No," said Harvey. "More like the pits."

"*Beautiful*," Jerry said, smiling and nod-
ding. Jerry always smiled and nodded when
he rapped with you, no matter what you
said.

"I hear you and Kate have it together
again and everything's cool, right? Listen,
you really did the right thing. When Jody
told me you were back at the house, you
know what I said? I said, 'Wow, Harvey's
back at the house.' That's just how I felt."

"Yeah, well, I appreciate that," Harvey
said.

"I mean, sure, what you did was really dumb and all that, but I don't believe in making value judgments." Jerry began inspecting Harvey's purchases. "You wanna get in on the car pool again? We've got a slot open if you want it, because Al Madison is very big on jogging these days and he doesn't ride with us anymore; he just sort of trots alongside."

"I don't think so," Harvey said. "I'm wired into Marin Transit right now, you know?"

"*That's* cool," Jerry said, "if you get off on buses. Hey ... you buying *Bonanza?* What are you trying to kill, the human race?" He took the Bonanza can out of Harvey's hand. "Listen, this stuff gets into the water table and you know what you've got? You've got *mutations.*"

"Yeah, okay. But right now what I've got is aphids."

"So you got aphids," Jerry said. "No *problem.* You mix up this superpowerful concentrate of garlic and water in the blender, see, and then you just get out there and put it on the veggies with your fingers. You don't need Bonanza; you got yourself one *dynamite* organic snuffer."

Harvey took the Bonanza back. "I guess I'm just a hunter-killer," he said. "Anyway, garlic never snuffed me, and I hang out a lot at Marin Joe's."

Jerry put down the wrought-iron baker's

rack he was carrying and jabbed Harvey in the collarbone with one finger, staring deeply into his sunglasses. "Harvey," he said, "I'm gonna tell you something upfront. Even if it means the end of this relationship. Like, this is going to be *brutal*, okay?"

"Okay," Harvey said.

"You tell me if I'm wrong here," Jerry said, "because I'm open to it. But I'm picking up this signal from you, you know what I mean? I mean *hostility*. Now, hostility's cool, you know? It's okay. But you wanna work through it, because *you are what you do*." Jerry paused. "Think about it, Harv."

Harvey thought about it. "I thought you were what you eat," he said finally.

Jerry shook his head. "Is that hostility," he said, "or is that *hostility*?"

Harvey dumped his peat moss, his Bonanza and his pulsator shower head on the counter at last and paid for the stuff with his Master Charge card. He didn't know why he was coming down on Jerry like that, and waited for him in the parking lot so he could make a gesture. "Listen, Jer," he said, "why don't we just leave all this stuff in your car and take my car and go get behind a beer at Sid & Jim's?"

Jerry smiled and nodded. "Can't do it, Harv," he said. "I gotta meet this dude and get my mantra." He slammed the door of his Rabbit hard enough so Harvey knew he was pushed out of shape.

Harvey decided to make the scene at Sid & Jim's anyway, although he should have been home by now changing into his wine-tasting clothes. The place was jumping, and he felt better after he'd ordered a Heineken's from a waitress who was a real throwback, an MCP's delight. Kate was over her granny dress and hiking boots phase, thank God, but she still wouldn't wear anything she considered "sexist," which meant anything he liked, so Harvey could really groove on a skirt slit up to the waist and platform shoes.

The waitress, in fact, looked a little like Marlene—the same long blond hair parted in the middle, the same terrific legs. Harvey wondered nostalgically if she, too, wore panties with days of the week printed on them.

It wasn't what Kate called "productive thinking," and Harvey tried to rise above it. He couldn't help feeling like kind of a schnook, though, when he thought about Marlene and that whole bit, because he'd never even tried to get in touch with her, after he'd split from the condo, just to make sure she was *coping*. What if she'd just freaked out entirely when she realized he wasn't coming back and O.D.'d on vitamin A or something?

Over the second beer from the same waitress, Harvey had a mind-blowing insight. Kate was always telling him how he had to "start taking responsibility instead of always copping out." She also said he had to "stop avoiding commitment" and that he wouldn't be a really mature person until he realized how immature he was.

And Kate was *right*. He saw it, because it was just *unreal* how he'd done it again. He had this responsibility, and the least he could do after copping out on Marlene like that was get in touch with her again and just offer to, like, be her *friend*.

He finished his beer, left the waitress most of his change, and headed for the pay phones downstairs. Maybe Marlene had told Sam Stein that night where she was going. . . .

20. Kate confronts Marlene

Joan's stereo was booming Montrose over half of southern Marin when Rita called, so even though Rita was practically screaming, Kate couldn't understand her. "Hang in there for a minute, will you?" she asked. "I've gotta go tell Joan to off that goddamn rock."

"I *can't*," Rita yelled. "They're here right *now*...."

"Who's where?"

"Marlene. Harvey's teenybopper. And Sam Stein. Listen, they're right here at Petrini's; it's just absolutely *wild*.... They just had this huge confrontation right in front of the freezer case, because Sam wanted to buy a Sara Lee streusel cake and Marlene said it was full of emulsifiers and she wouldn't even let him put it in the basket. She said it would *contaminate* the asparagus or something. And you wouldn't *believe* Sam.... He's wearing this *djellabah*—can you dig on it?"

"My God," Kate said. "I'm not ready for this. You know? I mean, I'm *simply not ready for this*."

"Yeah, well, you better get your act

together, like, right now," Rita shouted, "because Sam already walked out in this funk and Marlene's practically at the checkout. I think she's got nine items or less. . . ."

"I'm splitting right now, okay?" Kate hung up her Swedish phone with a sweaty hand. This wasn't the way she'd conceptualized the whole Marlene scene; furthermore, she wouldn't even have time to meditate before she confronted Marlene like one-to-one.

She hit 101 a minute later, wishing her sluggish VW bus were a Porsche and that she'd at least had time to change out of this square suburban sundress she was wearing because she'd been lying out on the chaise a few minutes ago working on tanning the back of her legs. You practically couldn't be caught dead in Petrini's without a good tan, for God's sake, and anyway, the sundress didn't project her real image. But there hadn't been time to put on her new wide-leg shorts from Foxy Lady or even to do her legs with Estée Lauder bronzing gel; she was just going to have to *come on* terrifically together.

Sam Stein wasn't with her, but Kate knew the tacky little chick in the wide-leg shorts was Marlene the minute she spotted her in front of the deli case, because Marlene looked just unbelievably *vacuous*. She was clutching a slip with a number on it in one hot little hand with Tickled Pink nail polish

on it and staring at the artichoke salad with big bovine eyes. Okay. Okay. Kate had to hand it to her. She had fantastic legs. But hadn't Harvey ever looked at her *face?*

Casually, Kate pulled down a number herself and sauntered up to a vantage point in front of the prosciutto. It was just incredible how freaked out she was: all this time she'd been thinking about how she was going to invite Marlene to La Caravelle or someplace, and then just tell her, woman to teenybopper, that she was bad news and that she had to stop coming on that way with types like Harvey and Sam because it wasn't *honest.* She was going to have this edge going for her because Marlene wouldn't know which fork to use and would never have heard of things like mussel salad.

Petrini's on Friday afternoon, though, was something else. First, it was terrifically public, with all those Ross types lined up at the registers to buy gin and cash checks. Secondly, although Kate was trying not to see it as a psychological advantage, Marlene even had a lower deli number than she did.

Remembering her assertiveness training, Kate approached Marlene on quivering sunburned knees. "Listen," she said, taking Marlene's dimpled little baby elbow in her own damp hand, "I wanna rap with you for a minute, okay? I'm Kate Holroyd. Harvey's *wife.*"

Marlene recoiled. She turned around to make eye contact. "Oh, wow," she said, gasping. "I can't *believe* this." She took in Kate's sundress, her macramé purse and her Bernardo sandals. "Oh, wow . . . I thought you were *fat*, you know?"

Kate was trying to come on laid back instead of unglued. "Marlene," she said, "you and I have to get clear, you know? Right upfront. I mean, you are into this incredibly *destructive* bag. First Harvey and now Sam Stein. I mean, do you have any *idea* of what you're doing to, like, *relationships?*"

To Kate's consternation, Marlene's eyes puddled up with tears. "Wow, this is so *heavy*, you know?" she said. "I mean, I can really relate to what you're saying. But it's not my fault. I mean, *really*. It's just terrible . . . the way men, like, exploit me. Like I told Harvey on the phone the other day, I can't help it if I've got this body, can I?" Marlene began to sob noisily. "Listen," she said urgently, "I'm a *person*, too. *Really. . .*"

Kate let go of Marlene's arm. "You told Harvey?" she asked incredulously.

"Yeah, well, he called me up," Marlene said. She blew her nose on a Kleenex she pulled out of the front of her halter top. "Like, on the phone. He said how he wanted to be my *friend* or something. Listen, he's even freakier than Sam, you know? And Sam's really a crazy. I mean, he's very big these days on 'overcoming his inhibitions,' and he reads all this stuff you wouldn't believe. And then he wants me to make it with him upside down on a trapeze or something. I'm not that kind of *person*...."

Marlene began to weep noisily again, but Kate wasn't registering. She just sort of stood there, feeling totally spaced, because the whole number was nothing short of *unreal*. When she thought of the way she'd trusted Harvey ... how she'd thought they'd finally got this terrific new openness going between them ... and now he was *acting out* again.

It blew her mind. In the meantime, Marlene was telling the man behind the deli case how she wasn't a sex symbol. He was listening intently, and so was everybody else in Petrini's. My God, this whole scene was practically out of *Ken Russell* or somebody.

"Listen," she said to Marlene, "there's one thing you have to remember. You're *okay*. Okay? I'm starting to flash on this whole bit, and you're right, it's not *your* fault." She put her arm around Marlene because Marlene was blowing her nose again and she just looked incredibly vulnerable, like a goddamn rabbit or something. "I mean, I'm gonna deal with this."

She tightened her grip and led Marlene firmly away from the deli counter, still clutching her paper number, and toward the parking lot. "Let's you and me go talk to Sam," she said grimly. "One to one. I mean, two to one. And I'll take care of Harvey for you, too, okay? You can *count on it*...."

21. Marlene is liberated

Bicycling home from the Sausalito ferry that Friday evening, Harvey hung a right into his driveway as usual and narrowly missed a head-on with Angela Stein's BMW 2002. He then registered Martha's old Rover parked at the curb and Ginger Gallagher's "Ross Volkswagen," a Mercedes four-door, across the street with its headlights still on. Three other cars that looked familiar were scattered along the block.

What the hell? Kate's women's group met Thursdays, so if they'd all made the scene at his place tonight, something *weird* had to be coming down. Had Germaine Greer joined Fascinating Womanhood or something?

Harvey walked his bike into the family room and chained it to the wall; not that he was heavily into private property, but anybody who ripped off his Motobecane was going to have to rip off the whole tract house with it. Then he headed for the living room, keeping his Bell helmet on just to be safe.

There he was practically blown away by the sight of Marlene sitting on his very own

Kroll sofa, surrounded by wads of Kleenex and Kate's entire support group, all of whom were staring at him with a look generally reserved for banana slugs and Bobby Riggs. Kate herself, enthroned in the Eames chair, was wearing what Harvey thought of as her "Joan of Arc at the stake" expression, but this time she was obviously already burned.

His first flash, a throwback to another age, was that Marlene was pregnant, although she didn't look it in those shorts and the halter top, even with nose red and her big eyes leaking steadily. Irrationally, Harvey remembered that he'd never got around to fixing that drip in the shower.

Harvey decided the best game plan was to stay loose. "*Well,*" he said cheerily. He

tried to smile, but it turned into a muscle spasm. "Ladies . . ."

Right away he knew he'd blown it, because the whole group stopped looking at him as if he were a banana slug. Banana slugs were at least alive.

"Did you *hear* that?" Ginger Gallagher asked everyone else incredulously. "I mean, my God, I can't believe I actually *heard* that."

"Oh, wow . . ." Marlene wailed. She blew her nose, and Martha put an arm around her. "This is really *heavy*, you know?"

"Harvey," Kate said, "sit down. And stop coming on with all that incredible crap. *Sit down*, Harvey."

Harvey sat down. "What crap?" he said.

Angela Stein threw her arms out helplessly, as if she were confronted with a native speaker of Urdu. "You know, Harvey," she said, "you are unreal. You are absolutely *not to be believed*—can you relate to that?"

"I'm easy," Harvey said. He wished he hadn't chained his bike to the wall, because they'd run him into the ground before he got the padlock off. For sure. "Hey, look, what's coming down here, anyway? I mean, I just sort of got here. I just got off my bike, you know? Maybe I ought to take a shower or something."

"What's coming down," Kate told him, "is that I just *happened* to meet *Marlene* in *Pe-*

trini's this afternoon, and she *told* me what
you and Sam Stein *did* to her. *That's* what's
coming down."

"Oh," Harvey said. "Yeah." He wondered
if Marlene had also shown movies.

"You *used* her, Harvey," said Kate's
friend Julie from macramé. "You exploited
her. You're, like, a *microcosm* of the whole
male power base. Don't you know that
macho number is *sick?*"

"I hear you, I hear you," Harvey said
sincerely. He was trying to remember the
enemy-avoidance techniques he'd learned
in Korea; could he pull off a combat crawl
out the patio door?

"Harvey," Martha said, "we love you, you
know? That's why we're here. That's what
you've gotta *grasp*. We really, *really* love
you. We wanna *help* you."

"Yeah, well, I'll feel a lot better after I've
had a shower," Harvey said. He made a
break for the hall, but Ginger Gallagher
threw a body block.

"No way," she said. "You can't run away
anymore, Harvey. Listen, you've gotta take
responsibility."

"I'm responsible," Harvey said. "Really.
You've got me all wrong, you know? I've
been working for Margaret Azevedo."

"Tokenism," Julie said. "Big deal."

"No, listen," said Harvey, "no tokenism. I
think she's really terrific. I think she oughta
be President. I mean, we oughta have a

woman President in this country, you know? Way overdue."

"Harvey," Kate said, "I hope you're more of a human being than Sam Stein. I mean, I'd really like to think you're a human *being*, Harvey. Do you know how Sam interrelated when Marlene and I, like, confronted him in Petrini's parking lot this afternoon? He copped out. He *split*. He was just sitting there, stoned out of his mind in these acid glasses and this *djellabah*, and he split. Did you ever hear anything so *dishonest*?"

"Never," Harvey said emphatically. "I know where you're coming from."

"So what are *you* going to do, Harvey? Where are *you* coming from?"

"I'm coming from the bank," Harvey said. Nobody laughed. "Hey, listen, couldn't we talk about this whole hassle, like, alone?"

"We are all ultimately, *ultimately* alone, Harvey," Kate said. "It's the human condition." Marlene began to cry noisily. "Anyway, the group and I have already rapped about this and we've done the really heavy problem-solving. Martha's going to take Marlene home with her, and she's joining the group. What we want from you is your *word* that you won't get in *touch* with her while she's trying to get in *touch* with herself—do you hear what I'm saying?"

"Sure," Harvey said. Kate was still looking at him as if she were figuring out which way to feed him into her Cuisinart. "Listen," he said to the whole group, "I'm very high on Bella Abzug, too. I heard Gloria Steinem at the College of Marin. *Terrific*."

"Hoo, *boy*," said Angela Stein. She came across the room and zeroed in on him. "Don't think you're headed for the showers yet, Harvey. You're the one that got Sam involved in this whole number, right?"

"Right," Harvey said.

"So you're the one that's gonna find him and bring him home. I don't want any *part* of Sam, naturally, but he's a very sick man—do you know what I mean?"

"Oh, yeah," Harvey told her. "Sam's really sick. I mean, he's sort of a microcosm of the whole male power base."

"So you go shower, Harvey," Kate said. "And then you can look for Sam. And listen, don't forget to take your helmet off. . . ."

22. Harvey finds Sam Stein

Kate was sitting out in the sun in the backyard in the lotus position when Harvey stuck his head out the patio door to tell her he was splitting. *"Please,"* she said. "I'm breathing."

Harvey waited until she came uncoiled. "I'm going to look for Sam again like you told me to," he said. "You know . . . search and destroy?"

"Listen, Harvey," Kate said coldly. "I don't think you're looking for Sam at all. I think you're just *coming on* like you're looking for Sam and what you're actually doing is hanging out. In bars."

"I'm looking for Sam in bars," Harvey said. "Really. That's where I'd be if I were Sam."

"Well, you're *not* Sam, Harvey," Kate said. She put her hands on her knees, palms up to catch the energy flow. "Has it ever occurred to you that you've got this terrific identity problem?"

"Sure," Harvey said. "All the time."

"So okay," Kate said, "that's your first priority, right? I mean, how do you expect to get your own head together jiving around drinking beer all the time? Why can't you just call Sam at the office?"

"I tried that. They said he wasn't heavily into urban planning just now and they didn't know when he'd make the scene again. He's on sick leave or something."

"I can relate to *that*," Kate said. "Sam's sick, all right. Listen, it still freaks me out what you and Sam did to Marlene, you know? I can't even concentrate on my mantra anymore."

"Yeah, well, I think I'll go look for old Sam," Harvey told her. He wasn't up for another Saturday-afternoon rap session about macho in Amerika. "I thought I'd sort of try the tennis club."

Kate turned around and looked at him. Squinting into the sun like that behind her shades, she reminded him of Brando in *The Godfather*. "Harvey," she said, "you *know* Sam isn't into tennis. Why can't you be honest with yourself?"

"He wasn't into djellabahs last time I saw him, either," Harvey said. "He's going through changes." He did a fast heel-and-toe out to the Volvo before Kate could pry herself out of the sidewinder of whatever the hell it was she was doing now and come slithering after him. Too bad he hadn't had time to grab his tennis racket, but you had to stay flexible; he could always drink beer.

When he flashed on Sam Stein, sitting in the gloom at the bar of The Velvet Turtle,

Harvey hardly recognized him. Here he'd been looking for a freak in acid glasses all these weeks, and Sam, with a haircut so short he had skin showing over his ears and wearing a polyester leisure suit, looked more like Bob Haldeman than Hunter Thompson. Sam was going through changes *for sure*.

Harvey picked up his Heineken's, wishing he could pick up the Terra Linda housewife in tennis whites at the end of the bar instead, and moved in on Sam. "Hey, good buddy," he said. (He'd been carpooling during the Marin Transit strike with a fellow banker who had a CB radio.) "Listen, there's an APB out for you, you know? I mean, Angela really wants you to make the scene in Ross again, and Kate sent me out to find you. I'm supposed to bring you back dead or alive; they've got this taxidermist all lined up. So whaddaya say?"

"Peace, Harv," Sam said serenely. He signaled for another gin and tonic. "Don't let it get to you."

"Sam," Harvey said, "you're not *listening* to me. What's coming down with you, anyway? I mean, why did you get your hair cut like that, with your ears sticking out? And the leisure suit. Leisure suits are *out;* they weren't ever in. Look, what are you trying to prove?"

"Leisure suits are *in* in Hammond, Indiana," Sam said. He paid for his g & t and offered Harvey the maraschino cherry. "I'm getting back to my roots, Harv, you know? I'm cutting out on Marin. They need urban planners in Hammond."

"Sam," Harvey said, "have you completely freaked out? Okay, so you're leaving Angela. That's cool; I mean, I know where you're at. But *Marin?* I mean, Jesus, you're leaving Marin for *Hammond, Indiana?*"

"Harvey," Sam said, "trust me. I know what I'm doing." He set down his drink with a shaky hand. "I can't take the whole Marin head-set anymore. Angela. Marlene. Natural foods. Cocaine. Woodacre. Flea markets. Pool parties."

"They don't have flea markets in Hammond?" Harvey asked. "They don't have pool parties? What's so goddamn oppressive about pool parties?"

Sam ate his maraschino cherry himself. "The last time we went to a pool party," he said slowly, looking straight ahead, "I went into the gazebo, and I *screamed,* Harvey. I flipped out. We were at the Gallaghers', you know, and Frank Gallagher fired up these outdoor speakers of his: Vivaldi, full throttle. So the Woodwards on the other side, they figured massive retaliation. They fired up *their* outdoor speakers: the overture from *Tristan und Isolde.*"

Harvey noticed that Sam had a tic going in his right eyelid. "Big deal," he said. "Listen, you ever been to Winterland? I

mean, noise is part of contemporary culture, you know? It's part of *life*."

Sam ignored him. He'd signaled for another g & t. "Then this guy on the next lot over—I guess he wasn't heavily into classical—he turned up these incredible Klips of his and he started playing Stan Kenton." Harvey noticed to his horror that Sam had tears in his eyes. " 'Artistry in Rhythm,' Harv," he said. "And that Japanese landscape artist with the Spanish-style across the street—he started playing 'Hawaii Calls.' He's got Klips, too. And Ginger Gallagher kept passing around organic prunes from the Torn Ranch, and Angela kept telling me how hurt she was because I didn't use the blow-dryer she bought me for Christmas, and everybody else was reciting bumper stickers and really getting off on 'We Brake for Garage Sales' and 'Another Glass-Blower for Udall' and 'Save the Wombats.' "

"Sam," Harvey said urgently, "get ahold of yourself, man." Sam's voice was rising alarmingly. "You wanna go to Hammond, go to Hammond. Whatever's right. . . ."

"Plant stores," Sam went on compulsively. "Kleen-raw in the hummingbird feeder. Weekends at Tahoe. *Vasectomies.* The Fungus Faire, redwood bathtubs, mandalas, compost piles, needlepoint, burglar alarms. . . ." Harvey had already begun to back toward the door when Sam's voice rose to a cracked tenor. *"Acupuncture, saunas, sourdough, macramé. . . ."*

Out in the parking lot, safely back in his Volvo with the doors locked, Harvey sat shaken. He hated to give her the satisfaction, but Kate was right. Sam Stein was really sick. . . .

23. Carol's empty closet

Kate flashed on Sylvia Schmidt right away, on the deck of La Veranda, while she was raising her blood sugar level with a plate of gnocchi. But she kept a low profile rather than going over to rap. For one thing, she was pretty sure the guy Sylvia was having lunch with was her ex-husband and she couldn't remember which one. For another, she and Harvey had just spent this weekend on the dinner-party circuit, and Kate, who'd gained four pounds on guacamole alone, had stepped on the scale this morning and got the bad news.

Of course she still wasn't exactly *gross*. It hadn't helped, though, that Harvey had appeared over her shoulder, watched the needle on the scale swing slowly to the right, shaken his head and hit her with, "Wow . . . Fat City."

So here she was, wearing her "fat dress," an ancient chemise now unfashionably short that left her piggy little knees hanging out, while Sylvia was wearing this throwaway-chic jumpsuit Kate had seen in Gigi's window on Friday and hadn't been able to zip when she tried it on. What was worse, the jumpsuit, a French import, had this size tag reading "42."

Okay, okay. She knew she shouldn't be munching out on carbos like this; substitute gratification wasn't the answer. Sylvia Schmidt was eating this austere green salad. But Sylvia didn't have a husband who put her down; she didn't have an ongoing husband at all. She had an A-frame on Panoramic with a sauna and a Jacuzzi instead of a Sutton Manor tract house with beer bottles full of rocks in the toilet tanks. She went to The Golden Door twice a year instead of squeezing in a week in a Tahoe motel, with a kitchenette and a black-and-white TV, at the wrong end of the lake. Sylvia had a together life.

Kate thought wistfully how Gloria Vanderbilt was right and you couldn't be too thin or too rich. She also speculated that Gloria Vanderbilt didn't have to practically live on Knudsen's lo-cal cottage cheese to keep from turning into Gargantua.

"I can't *believe* this," Sylvia said, when she saw Kate and came across the deck. "I mean, talk about your ESP. Wow, I was just picking you up on my radar, you know? Loud and clear. You must have a fantastic aura." She pushed her Dior shades down on her nose and looked over them at Kate's gnocchi. "Hey, I wish I could eat stuff like that. I just have to *look* at it, you know? . . . Fat City."

"I love your jumpsuit, Sylvia," Kate said. "Dynamite. Really."

"Oh, this. It's really old, you know? I keep on wearing it because Harry likes it, that's all; I mean, I figure it's the least I can do."

"Are you and Harry still tight?" Kate asked. "After the divorce and all? I mean, I'm kinda surprised."

"Kate," Sylvia said, "Harry and I can still relate to each other. Just because the relationship is over, that doesn't mean we can't have a *relationship*. Listen, why don't you come on over and hang out with us? You can bring that pasta or whatever it is along if you can lift it. Anyway, I've got something really heavy to lay on you. That's why I was picking up these vibes about you, you know? There aren't any accidents."

"Sylvia," Kate said warily, "I don't know if I'm ready for it. Harvey and I are going through this *dynamic* right now, and it's kinda where I'm at. I haven't got a lot of psychic energy left over for social interaction. So whatever it is, maybe you should just run it by me right here. Off the wall."

"I hear you," Sylvia said. She pulled up a chair, lit a Virginia Slim with her Dunhill lighter and flicked ash into Kate's plate. "Dig on this: *Carol's come out.*"

"Come out of what?" Kate asked, after a pause. "Her tube top?"

"Not to joke," Sylvia said. "She's *gay*. She's been seeing this terrific shrink, the one she used to get it on with, and he just, like, confronted her with it. He said she'd never stop sleeping around until she got up-front and came out of the closet. She told me about it at the Saturday Night Movie. In the *lobby*, can you believe it?"

"My God," Kate said. She was stunned. "How does she *feel* about it? I mean, can she get behind it?"

"She feels *incredible*," Sylvia said, blowing smoke. "She says she's finally gotten a handle on herself. It just hit her: she doesn't have to *fake it* anymore. With men."

Kate thought about the way Carol had faked it with Harvey a few months ago.

"Too bad," she said pointedly. "She had a class act going there."

Sylvia put her hand urgently on Kate's arm. She was wearing so many gold circle bracelets Kate was afraid their combined weight was going to make the deck collapse. "Kate," Sylvia said, "don't *do* this to yourself. You come on hostile and you're only hurting yourself, you know? You're interfering with your own *personal growth*."

Kate looked at her cold gnocchi. She looked at her round, bare knees. She wished Sylvia hadn't brought up "personal growth." "Okay," she said, "I'll call Carol. But what am I supposed to say to her?"

"You're *supposed* to tell her how you love her," Sylvia said. "How she's done this terrifically gutsy thing, and she's this beautiful human being, and you can really relate to where she's coming from."

"I know, but that's the *problem*," Kate said. "I mean, I hated Carol's guts when she was straight. Now I'm supposed to love her because she's gay? Isn't that, like, reverse discrimination or something?"

"Kate," Sylvia said slowly, "I think you should ask yourself why you feel so *threatened* by this. You know? You're overreacting, *really*." She stared significantly into Kate's eyes behind her shades. "Think about it. . . ."

Kate was outraged. She sat back and pried her arm loose. "Who, *me?*" she said.

"Listen, some of my best *friends* are lesbians. I mean, I haven't got any hangups about that stuff at all. I'm open to it. I'm easy."

"Kate," Sylvia said, "stop justifying yourself. You don't have to *justify* yourself with me. I mean, you just *are*, you know? Whatever's right."

"I'll call Carol," Kate said. "I said I'd call her and I'll call her, okay? Hey, Harry's waving his arms around. Maybe you ought to go back there."

Sylvia put out her cigarette and got up, shaking her head. "You really have to work on yourself, kid. You've got to stop thinking in terms like that. *'Ought,'* for God's sake. Don't you know there aren't any absolutes anymore?"

Kate wished Sylvia would self-destruct. "I'll talk it over with Carol," she said. "Okay? I mean, Carol should have a line on it. . . ."

24. At home with the Holroyds

"Why *can't* I have the bus?" Joan demanded over breakfast. "How come you get all the wheels around here, anyway? I mean, I've got rights, too, you know."

Kate tried to remember what their therapist had told her about really, *really* listening to Joan when she came on. "Of course you have rights," she said. "Doesn't she have rights, Harvey?"

"Yeah, sure," Harvey said. "Hey, listen, so do I. I have the right not to eat this goddamn granola every morning. Like, I'm a carnivore, you know? Why can't we ever have eggs and bacon in the mornings anymore?"

Kate sighed. "Harvey," she said, "you know eggs are full of cholesterol and bacon's full of carcinogens. You *know* that."

"I also know I've had it with granola," Harvey said. "I'm getting to the place where I'm gonna go out and kill, you know? For meat."

"I thought we were gonna talk about *my* needs for once," Joan said. "I mean just this once, okay? Spenser and I wanna split for Stinson this afternoon, and the Ferrari's broken down, and he's practically got to send off to Italy for a new carburetor or something. So why can't I have the bus? Gimme *one good reason*."

"One good reason is that I have a lunch date, sweetie," Kate said. She thought she was exercising a lot of restraint, but Joan wasn't having any.

"You call that a reason?" she asked. She rolled her eyes. "Don't you ever do anything but eat lunch with people, for God's sake? I mean, all you ever do is eat *lunch*, for God's sake. Listen, do you realize today is the first day of the rest of your life? I mean, how does that grab you?"

"Oh, boy," Harvey said. "That's really *profound*. We spend sixteen years raising this kid, and she opens her mouth, and what comes out? Bumper stickers."

Kate slammed the Melitta down on the Salton Hotray. "Will you *cool it?*" she complained. "I mean, why can't we ever have a dialogue in this household? Anyway, I *don't* exactly spend my whole life having lunch with people; a lot of my energies go into this household. I just cooked your breakfast, for starters."

"Granola isn't cooking," Harvey said. "It isn't *food*." He poked around in his bowl and then held his spoon up to the light. "What's in this stuff, anyway? Apricot kernels? Hey, Kate, I swear to you. I haven't got cancer. So never mind the Lae-

trile, okay? How about frying me an egg?
Like from a chicken?"

Kate took off her apron, the one with "For
This I Spent Four Years in College?" on it.
She snatched Harvey's granola bowl out
from under him and put it on the kitchen
floor for Donald the Afghan, who sniffed it
briefly and then crawled under the table in
the dining area. "Harvey," she said, "I
really think it's *time,* you know? I really
think it's time you learned to cope with
your anger. You are *incredibly* full of anger,
Harvey; when are you going to come to
terms with that?"

"I'm not full of anger," Harvey said. "I'm
full of granola. I'm trying to come to terms
with granola."

"So why can't I have the Volvo, then?"

Joan said to Harvey. "You don't want me to hitch, right? So you're gonna have to give me the car once in a while. It's only *logical*."

"Joan," Kate interrupted, in a voice that suggested patience strained to the breaking point, "how many times do I have to tell you not to brush your hair except in the bathroom? I mean, it's really *nice* that you want to be well groomed, but you get hair in the food. Hair in the food is a turn-off, Joan, sweetie. Anyway, you haven't got your license yet."

"Well, Spenser has *his* license." Joan glared at her murderously. "It says right on it, he can *drive*."

"Not my car," Harvey said firmly. "I don't lend my car to people with funny eyes. You ever look at Spenser's eyes? Spenser has wall-to-wall pupils."

Joan jumped up, shoving her hairbrush into the back pocket of her cutoffs. "Oh, boy," she said scathingly. "I really groove on your sense of humor, you know, Harv? Wow. You are *so* sick."

"I know," Harvey said. "I don't get enough eggs." He braced himself as Joan slammed the hall door. "Well," he said to Kate, "another mellow morning in Sutton Manor. Who are you having lunch with, anyway?"

Kate pointedly ignored Harvey's extended coffee cup. She sat down at the breakfast bar and stared at his left ear. "Harvey," she said, "do I open your mail?"

"I dunno," Harvey said. "Do you? Go right ahead, feel free. I open your Master Charge bills. Anyway, what's the mail got to do with it? You having lunch with your pen pal or something?"

"I am having lunch," Kate said regally, "with a *friend*. The point I'm trying to make is that I'm *entitled* to some privacy, you know? Even if we're married. I have my own identity, Harvey."

"Oh, sure," Harvey said. "Listen, I know where you're coming from. I just wondered where you're going."

Kate poured herself the last of the coffee. "Harvey," she said, "I'm going to tell you whom I'm having lunch with. But I'm warning you, I'm not into any more *scenes* this morning. Are we clear on that?"

"'Whom,'" Harvey said. "Wow. You're having lunch with a 'whom'?" Wait a minute, don't tell me." He closed his eyes tightly for an instant. "*Jerry Brown*," he said finally. "You got a hot answer back to that fan letter you wrote him. Look, I'm not gonna stand in your way, okay? I mean, you've got your own identity."

Kate leaned into Harvey's face, so closely he could feel her breath on his sideburns. The way she was looking at him, he flashed that she ought to have a collar with a bell on it.

"You *asked* for this, Harvey," she said. "Remember that. I'm having lunch with Carol, that's whom. Your ex old lady. Can you relate to that? I figure we have a lot to rap about, because for *some* reason Carol's off men these days—doesn't that psych you out? I mean, this I wanna *hear* about, you know?"

Harvey wondered where he'd put his un-der-the-seat flight bag the last time he went down to L.A. for the bank. "Sisterhood is powerful," he said weakly. "Listen, I've got a tennis date this morning. In Acapulco."

He was sitting in the Old Mill Tavern twenty minutes later pouring Cutty on the granola, thinking about Sam Stein and wondering if they also needed escrow of-ficers in Hammond, Indiana. Because good old Sam had really called the shots. What's more, Sam had got out of Marin, like, *in-tact*. . . .

25. Kate's lunch with Carol

"I can't go through with it," Kate told Martha on the phone. "I'm freaking. I can't even dig on what to wear, you know? I've been standing in front of my closet for *hours*, practically, just sort of *staring* at my clothes."

"So what's the problem?" Martha asked. "Okay, so you're having lunch with Carol. And Carol's come out. I still can't see why you can't even figure out what to put on your bod."

"Well, I thought if I wore my tap-dancing shorts, Carol might think I was coming on or something. And if I wore my Diane von Furstenberg, she might think I looked establishment and get negative vibes. And then I put on this yellow sundress ... you know my yellow sundress?"

"Sure," Martha said. "Dynamite."

"I'd forgotten about the neckline," Kate said. "It's terrifically low, you know? I thought Carol might think I was trying to make, like, a *statement*."

"Kate," Martha said wearily, "why don't you just wear your French jeans? You look terrific in pants. Really."

Kate let out a little cry of alarm. "I can't wear pants," she said. "I don't want Carol to think I'm *latent* or something."

"Look," Martha said, sighing, "it's quarter to twelve now, right? And you're supposed to meet Carol at Le Bistro at noon. So you're gonna have to get your act together and move on out. Wear your caftan. Carol can't pick up any signals if you're a coupla boy scouts in a pup tent."

"Oh, wow," Kate said. "You're right, you know? You oughta be a therapist or something. I mean, you have these incredible *insights*."

"Kate," Martha said, "I've gotta get back to my couscous, okay? You're not supposed to take your eyes off it, practically. So put on your caftan and split. And listen, call me back. I want a blow-by-blow."

"For sure," Kate promised. "*Ciao*, okay?"

She hung up the phone and bolted for her closet, wondering why she was coming unglued like this about having lunch with Carol, just because Carol was gay, when she didn't have any trouble relating to gay *men*. It was just like having lunch with Rudy, wasn't it, except that Carol didn't cut her hair?

Carol was waiting when she blew into Le Bistro, and after one look at her, Kate could have killed herself for being so uptight about this whole lunch number, because Carol, in a tie-dyed T-shirt and her I.

Magnin peasant skirt, looked terrifically *normal*. The same charm bracelet with the coke spoon on it, the same WASP afro, the same tinted Gloria Steinem shades with the little heart in the corner. What had Kate expected? Dress blues?

"Carol," she said, as she gathered up her caftan and squeezed behind the tiny table into a chair, "I wanna apologize, I really do. You wouldn't *believe* the changes I went through this morning. It made me realize how *rigid* I am. Deep down."

Carol shrugged. "I dunno what you're talking about," she said, "but it's okay by me. You wanna go through changes, go through changes." She leaned across the table and took Kate's hand. "Anyway, I'm the one that oughta apologize. About Harvey. I feel *terrible* about that whole scene, you know? Hey, Kate, it's beautiful of you to wanna get clear with me. You're so super upfront. I *love* it."

Kate jumped and pulled her hand away. "Oh, wow," she said immediately. "I'm *sorry*. I mean, it was a reflex or something."

Carol inspected her Juliette manicure. "Sure," she said. "Only I have this feeling, you know? I think you're having trouble, you know, *relating*. Listen, Kate, I'm not any different. I'm just *different*. Like, I'm the same person and everything."

Kate contritely put her hand back on the table in case Carol wanted to squeeze it again. "Carol," she said, "you really are too much. I mean, you're just terrific, you know? You're giving off this *incredible* togetherness. It's beautiful."

Carol nodded absently. Kate noticed with some confusion that behind her shades, Carol's eyes were following this macho waiter around the room. *"That* figures," Carol said. "I'm in touch with my essence. Boy, I dunno how I'm ever gonna thank Lloyd enough for putting me straight. I mean, you know what I mean. He's the one that flashed on how I was plugged into this 'anatomy is destiny' crap, and how I was sleeping around all the time because I thought I had to *prove* something. Listen, I mean he *really* blew me away."

"Yeah, I'll *bet*," Kate said. She couldn't figure out why Carol was tracking the waiter like that. "But I still don't exactly see the connection. What does all that stuff have to do with being, you know, gay?"

Carol looked at her as if she wasn't exactly high on Kate's smarts. "Look," she said, "it's simple. You really come to terms with being a woman and you're gonna relate to women. I mean, who needs men? What do you need Harvey for, for instance? What does *anybody* need Harvey for?"

Kate wished Carol wouldn't back her up against the wall like that. "Well," she said earnestly, "Harvey's got a lot of good points, he really does. He grows terrific tomatoes.

And this year he gave me *Our Bodies, Ourselves* for our anniversary, which I thought was really progress, because last year he gave me this Waring blender. Don't you think that shows he's, like *trying?*"

Carol chortled. "Oh, yeah, Harvey *tries,*" she said. "For sure. Harvey's always trying."

Kate put her hand back in her lap again. "Carol," she said, "why are you being so hostile? I mean, I get this feeling like you're *hostile.* What are you trying to prove?"

"I'm trying to *prove,*" Carol said stiffly, "that you don't have to *define* yourself through Harvey, okay? Like, life is a *menu,* you know what I mean? You've got your choice of soup or salad."

Kate gathered up her caftan and got to her feet. "Yeah, well," she said furiously, "I don't think I'm ready to order, you know? And listen, you shouldn't *generalize* like that. About men. All generalizations are false."

"Sure," Carol said languidly. "You ever see it rain *up?*"

At home in her tract house, Kate got on the phone to Martha again. "I'm sorry to dump on you like this," she said, "but it couldn't even wait for group. That's how bummed out I am."

"Kate," Martha said soothingly, "it's all process, okay? Listen, though, that reminds me. I wanna regroup the group. I've got this *fantastic* idea. . . ."

26. According to the contract

Martha tackled Bill about her marvelous idea on a tranquil Fairfax afternoon when Tamalpa and Che, her two children from previous marriages, were off to the planetarium with the rest of Waldorf School and Bill's son Gregor was visiting his mother. She put Joni Mitchell on the stereo, served him herbal tea with eucalyptus honey in it and put a plate of her homemade zucchini bread between them on the redwood slab coffee table. She wanted to create the right ambience.

Bill heard her out with a wary look. "Martha," he said, when she'd finished, "run that one by me again slowly, will you? I thought the whole point about your women's group was, you know, sisterhood. So how come you want me to come? And Harvey Holroyd? And what's-his-name, that poodle-groomer Angela Stein's hanging out with? What are we supposed to do, show up in drag?"

Martha sighed. She liked to think of Bill as a spiritual partner instead of a husband, so it bothered her that instead of being on the same wavelength, he was sending out a lot of static. If she hadn't known better, she'd have thought he was threatened.

"Paco," she said. "His name's Paco. He's Argentinian—isn't that far out? And he's not really a poodle-groomer; he's an artist. He does, like, happenings, but there isn't much happening in the field right now. Anyway, sweetie, you're not really *listening* to me, you know?"

Resigned, Bill gave up on the All-Star game; Martha wouldn't let him have the TV in the living room anyway, because she thought it was tacky, but he still got his hopes up once in a while.

"No, really," he said. "I hear you, babe; I just can't figure out what space you're in. Like, I'm just not in the same place, you know what I mean?"

"Bill," Martha said earnestly, "what do you think we rap about all the time in the group? *Think* about it."

"Men?" Bill asked. It wasn't really a question.

Martha looked pleased. "Oh, wow, you're so *right*," she said. "I mean, we also rap about what it means to be female and all, but we're really talking about what it means to be *human*. You know—sex-role stereotyping, identity, meaningful human relationships. The whole gestalt. So I had this flash. I thought, wow, what if we got the men *involved?* We could have this terrifically productive dialogue."

"Sure. Or a really terrific massacre." Bill decided to win through intimidation. "Look, Martha, I can't really dig on this whole number, and I'll bet Harvey and Frank Gallagher and all those good old boys aren't exactly going to get off on it either. So why don't you just invite Pablo? He's the one that's into happenings."

"*Paco*," Martha snapped. "I told you, you're not *listening* to me. Listen, don't you realize if you're not part of the solution you're part of the problem?"

"Not necessarily," Bill said. "That's simplistic."

"Of course it's simple," Martha told him. "What I can't understand is, why didn't I *see* it until now? I guess I've had a lot on my mind, sort of a psychic overload or something. But I'm feeling a lot more up-beat about Gregor now that I've talked the whole scene over with Vivian. She says all kids his age set fire to stuff and we should just sort of give him more attention and not make a big deal out of it. You think we oughta at least install a smoke detector?"

Bill choked on his tea. He set the mug down carefully. "Aren't you getting awfully tight with Vivian these days?" he asked Martha.

Martha pounded him harder than necessary between the shoulder blades. "Bill," she said, "just because Vivian's your ex, that doesn't mean she can't be our friend. I mean, I think Vivian's terrific. *Really*. And she is Gregor's biological parent, even if he does relate to me. Anyway, Naomi's got this theory; she thinks Gregor plays with matches because he senses, you know, all this tension about the divorce."

"Yeah, well, I happen to hate Vivian's guts," Bill said. "*I've* got a lot of tension about the divorce for sure. So cool it with Vivian, okay?"

Martha moved serenely across the Rez-aian rug and turned Joni Mitchell over to the flip side. "I can't cool it with Vivian," she said, "because it wouldn't be *cool*. Listen, everybody's loose about exes these days. It's *healthier*. Bill and Frannie and Joanne and Chuck take *saunas* together, for

God's sake. So why are you so hung up about Vivian?"

"I'm not hung up about Vivian," Bill said belligerently. "I'm not hung up. I've been through psychoanalysis *twice*, remember?"

Martha poured them each more tea, cut a slice of zucchini bread and thought to herself how men were just like children sometimes. "Bill," she said sweetly, "I don't think you're really in touch with your feelings about this, you know? Vivian doesn't think so either; she's gonna come to group, too, though, so you can get down and work through it. Really get clear."

Bill stared at her for a moment, left the room, went to their Espenet desk and came back waving a handful of onionskin. "Martha," he said triumphantly, "I don't have to go along with this whole scene and you can't make me. It's not in the marriage contract. Okay? I just read the whole thing over again. So forget it."

Martha shook her head. "Wow, I can't *believe* this. You know that contract is just a general agreement. Just a sort of broad overview. I mean, it's not exactly words to live by or anything. Boy, talk about your copout . . ."

"Yeah, well, that's not the way you interpret it when it's time to take the garbage out," Bill said vehemently. "Listen, Martha, I'm not going through with this. *No way*. I'm not gonna go to your women's group with you and Vivian. I'm gonna talk this whole thing over with my *attorney*."

Martha was determined to stay laid back. "You're overreacting, Bill, sweetie," she said. "So we'll deal with all this later, okay? But I think you should know. Vivian and Carl are adding on to their house. They're building a *sauna*—are you ready for that? And listen, that reminds me—because I was just thinking it's about time for Gregor to make the scene. Have you seen my Dunhill lighter?"

27. Boys and girls together

The first meeting of the regrouped consciousness-raising group took place at the Holroyds' and was launched by Martha's suggestion that they all "just sort of turn inward for a moment and silently celebrate their womanhood."

Straight away, Harvey embarrassed Kate. Since he and Frank Gallagher and Martha's Bill and Angela's friend Paco were biologically unqualified to celebrate their womanhood, he suggested, maybe they could "just split for the 2 A.M. Club and have a quick beer while the girls turn inward."

Kate wasn't amused. "Harvey," she said coldly, "it wouldn't hurt you to try to *relate* for once. That's why we're here, you know? To really get down and relate. Anyway, the beer bit is *out*. Alcohol alters your perceptions. Like, it gets between you and reality."

"Yeah," Harvey said, sighing. "I know." But the way Kate and the rest were looking at him, he decided he'd better not make waves. "Okay. I'll just sort of sit here and celebrate my womanhood. I mean, I'll try to

relate. You think it would help if I combed
my hair?"

Frank Gallagher chuckled, but then he
got this look from Ginger and copped out.
"Wow, I'm sorry," Frank said. "I just can't
help it. I'm a Leo. We're all very big on
macho tripping. But I'm trying to, like, overcome it."

"Fink," said Martha's Bill viciously, under his breath. Harvey thought Bill looked
just about as bummed out as he was. All
week long he'd been trying to psych himself up for this whole scene, but by five
o'clock this afternoon the prospect of discussing what Kate called his "honest
emotions" with the Weird Sisters had him
so freaked he'd primed himself on three
martinis at Paoli's before he'd biked home.

Did Kate realize what happened to your reflexes when you rode a ten-speed on three martinis? Halfway down the grade into Sausalito, Harvey had had this *mano a mano* with a Langendorf bread truck he was sure had his number on it. Was raising his consciousness worth lowering his odds?

At least his worst nightmares hadn't come true. Marlene, the group's biggest success story, hadn't been able to make it tonight because, Kate told him, she was beginning Leonard Orr's Theta seminars and didn't want to miss anything. Marlene said Theta taught you how to overcome Specific Negatives like "hangups and physical death."

It sounded A-okay to Harvey, who wondered if Leonard Orr could teach him how to overcome specific negatives like Kate and her support troops. He wondered how Martha's Bill related to sitting on the sofa between Martha and his ex-wife Vivian. He wondered whether Vivian held her big floppy hat on with a hatpin.

He was wondering, too, if he could get away with faking an onslaught of swine flu, when he realized the moment of silence was over and Kate was going around the room offering everybody green tea and those freaky little noshes she picked up at the Japanese Trade Center. "Sushi?" Kate kept saying brightly.

Frank Gallagher and all the women took

some, but when Bill said he "punched out at raw fish," the sushi hit the fan. "Bill," said his ex-wife Vivian, "you just reminded me of something, sweetie. You just reminded me how closed you always were to experience, you know? Why don't you just open up? Why don't you make yourself *vulnerable*?" She put her hand with the long Liza Minnelli fingernails on his arm. "Listen, Bill, sweetie, you can eat raw fish and still be a man, don't you realize that?"

Bill wheeled around on the sofa. "That's a crock, Vivian," he snapped. "Anyway, what do you know about 'vulnerable'?" He turned to Angela Stein's Argentinian poodle-groomer, who plucked nervously at the creases in his leather suit. "Vivian here is about as vulnerable as the Corps of Engineers—you know what I mean?"

Paco smiled and nodded under his pompadour. "*Pleese?*" he said.

"Listen, Bill," Angela said promptly, "Paco's *very* sensitive about his English. In fact, he's very sensitive. So get off his case, okay? You don't have to come on like such a heavy."

"He didn't come on like a heavy," Harvey said. "He said he punched out at raw fish. So what's the problem? I can't get behind sushi either, you know? I'm boycotting Japanese food till they stop killing whales."

"Harvey," Ginger Gallagher said, "I think we'd better lay down some ground rules about now, okay? And rule number one is *no power tripping*. Nobody needs power tripping, Harvey. So you can just forget that head-honcho number you're trying to pull. You know very well Vivian wasn't talking about sushi; sushi's just a *metaphor*. Isn't that right, Paco?"

"*Pleese?*" Paco said. Harvey noticed that Paco's black-bean eyes were fixed on Kate, who had frozen in front of him with her Cost Plus lacquer tray. He also flashed that Kate was staring back at Paco like a deer in front of somebody's headlights.

"Sure, I hear you, Ginger," Harvey told her. "Wow, that's terrific, what you said. About how sushi's a metaphor. I always thought of it as, you know, raw fish?"

This time Martha took him on. "Harvey," she said too sweetly, "don't you realize Vivian is trying to *help* Bill? That's what we're here for. To help each other."

Harvey was beginning to realize his back was to the wall. He looked at Frank Gallagher, but Frank had gone over to the other side and was practically licking Ginger's hand. He looked at Bill, but Bill was engaged in heated debate with his ex-wife about which of them was the flake. "Hey, Kate," Harvey finally called weakly, "I could use a little help over here. Hey, Kate, baby?"

Kate didn't hear him. She was still standing there clutching her lacquer tray like Madame Butterfly and staring at Angela Stein's Latin poodle-groomer, who Harvey thought looked like something out of a Tubes concert.

"Paco," he heard her saying slowly, through the growing uproar in his living room, "do you ever clip Afghans? *Afghans?*"

Paco looked up at her meltingly. His suit creaked as he reached for a piece of sushi, swallowed it whole without ever taking his eyes off Kate, and licked his fingers.

"Pleese . . ." Paco said.

28. Kate's new playmate

Ms. Murphy kept Marlene on "Hold" for twenty minutes before she finally told Harvey his "chick from the checkout stand" was on the line. "You wanna rap with her," Ms. Murphy asked, "or should I just, like, tell her her account's closed?"

Harvey considered. Kate and her consciousness-raising group had made it clear as liquid crystal that he wasn't supposed to communicate with Marlene privately. *No way*. Further, he was into the simple life these days. But he couldn't let Ms. Murphy manipulate him, so he told her to put Marlene through instanter. "She probably wants some advice about money or something," he said.

Ms. Murphy snorted. "Yeah," she said, "for sure. Hey, listen, am I right or am I right? I get this feeling she's a Virgo. Like, it's just this feeling I get."

Harvey conceded that Marlene was a Virgo. "I *knew* it," Ms. Murphy said with satisfaction. "Listen, Virgos are bad news. You wanna stay clear, you wanna go with your water signs."

Harvey picked up the phone. "I can't

swim," he said. "You got out that letter I gave you this morning, or are you permanently out to lunch?"

Ms. Murphy sauntered out of his office with the walk that was one reason he kept a secretary who thought typing was a bummer. The other reason was his fear that like Elizabeth Ray, she might be writing her memoirs. "Don't get uptight," Ms. Murphy said, as a parting shot. "You get uptight and my typewriter freaks. It picks up vibes, you know?"

"Harvey," Marlene said, while he was still wondering why women took turns working him over these days, "what's coming down? Like, I wondered how you were, you know, swinging with the Third World? You keeping your cool?"

"You mean not buying grapes?" Harvey said, mystified. "Well, I can take or leave grapes. It's no big thing."

Marlene sighed. "Harvey," she said, "you really are too much. Wow, I should've known you'd come on like this. Don't you ever let yourself *feel*, Harvey?"

"Sure I let myself feel," Harvey told her. "Listen, I rode in the Marin Century last weekend. One hundred miles on the old Motobecane. You better believe it, it still hurts when I laugh."

Marlene sighed heavily again. "Harvey, I'm gonna be upfront with you. I mean, I know you don't like it when a person is upfront, but I don't get off on games anymore. I'm in a whole nother space. And anyway, I still *care* about you. I can't help caring about you, because I'm a people person."

"Terrific," Harvey said. "Marlene, I swear to you. Cesar's my main man. I'm not holding, okay? *No grapes.*"

Marlene waited him out. "Harvey," she said, "you've gotta know, because you've gotta learn to get behind pain. Really go with it. But I don't want you to make any value judgments."

"Hey, listen, Marlene, I've gotta sign this letter, so why don't you just sort of, you know, spit it out?" He figured it must be Marlene's turn to work him over and was immediately proved right on.

"Kate is just incredibly *committed* to another relationship," Marlene said. "Can you relate to that? She told us about it in group. She wanted to tell you about it, so she could *share* with you, but you were off riding your tricycle or something. Anyway, she's living with this terrific anxiety. She's afraid you're still hung up on the double standard. In the seventies, Harvey. In *Marin County.*"

Harvey stared at the yellow light on his telephone. He tried to go with it. "Who's Kate getting it on with?" he said finally. He thought he sounded very Marin County in

the seventies, but Marlene apparently
didn't.

"Wow, don't *be* like. that, Harvey," she
said. "*Who* is not the *point*. The point is
that Kate is really, *really* happy, you know?
And she wants to share, because she wants
you to be happy *with* her. Listen, haven't
you even read *Open Marriage* yet?"

"No," said Harvey. "I'm still finishing
Meter Maids in Bondage. Who's Kate getting it on with? I mean, who is she incredibly committed to?"

"That's not the *point*, Harvey," Marlene
insisted again. "You're missing the whole
point."

"No, I'm not. I wanna share. How can I
share if I don't know who she's getting it on
with?"

"Harvey," Marlene told him sweetly,
"I'm gonna hang up now. But I feel really
good about this whole conversation. I want
you to know that. Because I know you're
gonna get your head straight when you
mellow out and take the overview. And
remember, you promised. No value judgments . . ."

Harvey's strongest impulse, when he
stopped flashing on feeding Marlene
through the Wells Fargo shredder, was to
split for the house and confront Kate. But he
had this sudden image of himself wheeling

into the drive to defend the double standard, in his Bell helmet and his cycling shoes with the pointy toes, and it didn't do much for him. So he settled for an instant replay instead.

What was that bit about him "swinging with the Third World"? Had Kate and her cellmates joined the PLO? Had she caught a late-night rerun of *Viva Zapata* again? Was she getting it on with a waiter at Don Pancho's?

When it hit him, it blew him away. Why hadn't he put it together?

Kate had mentioned recently that she thought she'd sign up for night classes in Spanish at the College of Marin because she was tired of being "a WASP imperialist." Their Afghan, Donald Barthelme, had been clipped so many times in the last few weeks he didn't look like a dog anymore. And just last night, over dinner, Harvey'd filed a complaint that Kate's ratatouille smelled like disinfectant instead of eggplant.

His wife was getting it on with that hokey Latin poodle-groomer of Angela Stein's, the one with the styled-out leather suit and the guacamole accent. So what was Harvey supposed to do, challenge Paco to a salsa contest?

29. Coping with adultery

Ten years ago, finding out that Kate was getting it on with another man, while not exactly a piece of cake, would have been something Harvey could have handled. First he would have done his imitation of Genghis Khan. Then he would have forgiven Kate and allowed her to spend the rest of her life making it up to him.

Ten years ago wives were wives, rather than women, and "affirmative action" was popping them right in the orthodontia when they stopped baking chocolate-chip cookies in their spare time and started screwing around.

Now, however, it wasn't that simple. Wife-beating, in Marin in the seventies, was considered a crime against humanity second only to lighting a cigarette in a crowded elevator. Not only couldn't Harvey shake Kate until she lost her contact lenses; he couldn't even close her charge accounts.

None of his alternatives, in fact, seemed viable; none of them would survive a feasibility study; and none of them, he was sure of it, would make it through the Mill Valley Planning Commission. Standing at the rail of the Sausalito ferry on his commute home, Harvey decided his only real option was to get bombed out of his skull; some things never went out of style, thank God, and Cutty on the rocks was one of them.

He didn't even flash on Ms. Murphy, standing at his elbow, until she rested half of her "Tower of Power" T-shirt on his wrist, right over his Pulsar watch. "Hey," she said, as Harvey nervously pried loose under the guise of looking to see what day it was. "Mr. Escrow Department himself. Boy, you really look like you're in the pits, you know? I mean *the pits*. Whatsa matter, you got a flat in one of your sew-ups again?"

"Thanks, I needed that," Harvey said. "Listen, you wanna tell me what's coming down with me and women these days? I've got this feeling. Like maybe *Ms.* has a contract out on me or something. You wanna be the hitperson, too? Get in line."

Ms. Murphy sighed as she settled herself over his wristwatch again. "Harvey," she said reproachfully, "you're unreal. Wow, you're practically a paranoid's paranoid. What's *bugging* you, man?"

Harvey swallowed the rest of his double Cutty with his free hand. "What's bugging me," he repeated, "is my wife's getting it on with this banana republic Paul Newman with a dog beauty parlor. Marlene called this afternoon and worked me over. And

right now, you happen to be lying on top of my watch. I mean, I can't even tell what time it is, you know?"

"Oh, man, I *hear* you," Ms. Murphy said, shaking her head. "I really, *really* hear you. Boy, I can just *imagine* the space you're in." She began to massage the back of Harvey's neck. "Now listen, Harv . . . you gotta stay loose, you know? Hang in there; go with it; you can't beat it, join it."

"Sure," Harvey said. "You been reading the *Desiderata?*"

Ms. Murphy looked confused. "Is that by Rod McKuen?"

Harvey decided he needed another drink and muscled his way back to the ferry bar, where martinis were selling like tickets to *A*

Chorus Line. There he ordered another double despite Ms. Murphy, who seemed to have joined herself to him at the hip and who urged him to take "*massive* doses of megavitamins" instead because he was "undergoing a crisis reaction."

"So what's my next move?" he asked her, when they were back at the rail contemplating Marvelous Marin across the water. "Go after Paco with his own clippers? You better believe it, I'm ready."

"*Negative*," Ms. Murphy said emphatically. "Not unless you wanna end up in the slammer, Harv. Look what they did to Inez Garcia."

Harvey noticed that he couldn't see his Pulsar again. He also noticed that Ms. Murphy was breathing heavily, giving off little puffs of Binaca. "You got a better idea?" he asked.

Ms. Murphy shifted slightly so that Harvey got the whole Tower of Power. She wrapped a moist hand around his ear and whispered into it, and what she told him made Harvey stagger in his Earth Shoes. Apparently Ms. Murphy read not only Rod McKuen but early Henry Miller, with a little Marquis de Sade on the side.

When he recovered from his initial crisis reaction, Harvey agreed to sprint for her place when the boat docked and meet her there, Ms. Murphy declining to run alongside his bicycle. He also decided, since he'd opted for massive retaliation, to call Kate from the Valhalla on the way and tell her, right upfront, that as far as he was concerned, their interface was over—*finito*.

Granted, as Kate kept reminding him, she wasn't his property, and although he paid for maintenance, he couldn't deduct depreciation.

True, he'd been the one to open up their marriage; but he'd only intended to open it up halfway, and that was *his* half.

And finally, Harvey wasn't an equal-opportunity employer. If Kate wanted to run with Paco and the dog pack when she was off duty, she could get herself another job. Maybe she could find happiness reading meters for PG&E.

When he made the call, he got his daughter Joan instead of Kate. "Don't *yell* at me, Harvey," Joan screamed, when he tried to outshout the Klips in the background. "I can't relate to yelling. And anyway, Kate's not home. She split. She said she was going away for the weekend and you knew all about it.... Listen, I can't *hear* you when you mumble, okay?"

Harvey tried to modulate between a mumble and a roar. It wasn't easy, because he had this mental image of Kate packing her overnight bag, with the nightgown he'd given her for Christmas last year right on top.

"Into the woods," Joan said. "She said

she was going into the woods or something. Listen, you don't have to yell at me, Harvey. I mean, where do you think I am? Winterland?"

Harvey hung up and made his unsteady way back to the Valhalla parking lot. Ms. Murphy was waiting for him, but now that he thought about what she'd whispered in his ear, the prospect freaked him out. What was that bit about her two roommates and an SX-70? And did he remember correctly, in his double-Cutty haze, that she also had plans for his bicycle? . . .

30. Kate dumps on Martha

"Martha," Kate said, "I hope you don't feel I'm *using* you or anything. Because I don't get off on *using* people, really. But I had to dump on somebody, you know?"

"Sure," Martha told her. "I know just where you're coming from." She also wondered wearily if Kate was on a one-way trip. She'd been unburdening herself, over half a gallon of Foppiano Chablis and homemade carrot cake, for hours, practically, and while Martha was trying to remain supportive, her eyes were starting to glaze over.

"You're beautiful, Martha, you know?" Kate squeezed Martha's hand warmly, oblivious to the fact that it held a piece of carrot cake. "Anyway, I've *never* seen Harvey so freaked out. Not in all these years of living with a paranoid. *Nunca.*"

"*Nunca?*"

"That's Spanish for 'never.' I'm taking this night class, didn't I tell you? *Anyway,* you should have seen the house when I trucked into the driveway Sunday night. Harvey had all these lights on. I mean *all*

the lights. ... Wow, it looked like a nuclear reactor or something."

"Kate," Martha said, digging carrot cake out from beneath her fingernails, "didn't you, like, tell Harvey where we were going before you split on Friday? About the Women's Weekend in the Country?"

"Martha," Kate said, exasperated, "I gave him the total picture. Honestly. Only when I got home, he'd forgotten or something. He was just *insane*. I mean, he'd been wandering around the streets in Sausalito all night Friday and Saturday, just worrying about me. So the *next* thing I know, he hits me with this incredible number about how I wasn't up in Mendocino at all. I was *actually* getting it on with Paco in Tijuana or someplace. Isn't that freaky? Isn't that *out-rageous?*"

"*Loco,*" Martha said.

"I mean, even when I showed him this receipt for the workshops I took . . ." She paused, impressed. "Hey, I didn't know you spoke Spanish."

"Listen, how did you groove on the Weekend?" Martha asked. She was trying to change the subject, although she couldn't remember, just at the moment, what it was. "I hardly even zeroed in on you, you know, because you were taking Chainsaw and Tai chi and I spent both days in Auto Repair."

Kate squeezed her hand again. Again it was full of carrot cake. "Chainsaw was *fabulous,*" she exclaimed. "I mean, Tai chi was okay. But *Chainsaw* . . . Wow, I was so freaked out about it at first, you know? But then it gave me this terrific buzz. . . ."

Why was Kate now dumping the contents of her macramé bag out onto the natural linen sofa? Martha was suddenly so zonked on Foppiano, she was afraid she might be hallucinating. Big Red pen, Gucci wallet and change purse, natural-bristle brush, Zig Zag papers and a can of flea powder. "You looking for something?" she asked blearily.

"I'm out of matches," Kate said. "What have you done with your Dunhill, anyway?"

Martha stiffened. While Gregor's therapist felt he was definitely "pulling away from his incendiary tendencies," Martha had her doubts. Not only was her Dunhill still missing after several weeks, but so was the butane for her chafing dish, their automatic charcoal lighter and her soldering iron for jewelry making. And a furtive search of Gregor's room, a violation of his civil rights, had produced nothing more than his collection of stills from *Deep Throat*.

"I'm not into smoking these days," she lied. "Listen, why don't you just go down and rent a chain saw at A to Z? Give Harvey a demonstration?"

"I can't," Kate said. "I thought of that myself, but Harvey saw this movie—*The Texas Chainsaw Massacre*. So I mentioned it to him and he just wigged out. Anyway, don't you have to have a permit or something from the Sierra Club?"

Martha noticed that she couldn't separate her two middle fingers. They seemed to be glued together with carrot cake. She also found, when she tried to stand up, that her motor coordination seemed to be shot. Not that she had to *prove* anything . . .

"Look, I don't wanna manipulate you or anything," she enunciated carefully to Kate, "but if you wanna tell me something, you better tell me. Because I just noticed. I'm really bombed." Was Gregor home from school yet? She couldn't remember.

"You can't be bombed," Kate said airily.

"Not on wine, Martha, sweetie. Wine's organic. It's made from *fruit*."

Martha made a last attempt to pry her fingers apart. "Kate," she demanded, "I'm gonna ask you something right upfront. Are you getting it on with that dude with the dog parlor or not?" Kate swam before her in double focus. One of her contact lenses floated eerily off to the side on what Martha realized were tears.

"Well," Kate said, "sort of. I'm *sort* of getting it on. But I'm not exactly getting it *on*. Paco's fantastic at nonverbal communication, but there's still this language barrier. And Angela Stein." She stuffed her wallet and her Zig Zags back into her purse, her face flushing. "The bummer is that Angela's got the dogs."

"She's got the *what?*" Martha was flashing on something weird, just at the edges of her remaining consciousness, but she was too far gone on fruit to get in touch with it.

"The dogs," Kate wailed. "He has to have dogs, you know? To clip. And Angela knows all these heavy-duty dog freaks, and she keeps sending them to Paco, and all I've got is Donald Barthelme. I mean, I know Paco loves me, but he can't keep clipping the same damned dog all the time, because there isn't any *percentage* in it for him, you know? Sure, Donald's a big dog. But there isn't anything left on him to clip."

Martha noticed that her eyes were watering. She knew it wasn't empathy, because she hadn't been able to track on what Kate was rapping about for the last two hours. She also noticed that her copper bracelet was becoming uncomfortably warm. "Kate," she asked abruptly, "do you smell smoke?"

Kate wrinkled her nose and sniffed the air. "Well, *sort* of," she said. "I *kind* of smell smoke."

Martha lurched to her feet and began to pull Kate unsteadily across the Oriental and toward the front door. "We're gonna go outside for a while, okay?" she said. "Not to panic or anything. But I have this freaky feeling." Down in the valley, below her Fairfax Canyon A-frame, she heard the sirens. "I think I just found my Dunhill. . . ."

31. Kate's surprise haircut

Kate was having her hair cut at Shear Ecstasy, nervously watching Mr. Donald snip away at her bangs, when she saw Carol's back appear briefly in the mirror that ran the length of the room. She knew it was Carol's back because Carol was wearing her classic '74 Nik-Nik shirt, the one with the Art Deco garden party on it in muted shades of orange, lavender and puce.

Nik-Nik had traded in Art Deco for M. C. Escher geometrics this season and Kate thought the new line was a little tacky. But Carol, whose sense of fashion was timeless, intuitively clung to her oldie-but-goodie. Carol believed in basic decadence.

Mr. Donald, sleek as a trout in his high-waisted bell bottoms, was holding up a handful of Kate's hair in his manicured fingers. "Honestly," he said to her image in the mirror, "I just can't *believe* what's happened to your hair since I did you last time. It's practically *screaming* for protein. And the sides ... they look like crab grass. Who *did* this to you, anyway?"

Kate didn't have the courage to tell Mr. Donald that he'd cut her hair last time, too, because you had to be careful with hairdressers. Years ago, she'd argued with one of Mr. Donald's predecessors, about the farmworkers' strike or something, and when he'd got through wielding his scissors, she'd walked out of the shop looking like John Glenn. "Jesus," Harvey had said, when she came tearily in the door and took off her scarf, "you going out for basketball or something?"

"Well," she now confessed to Mr. Donald timidly, "I sort of trimmed it myself. I mean, I couldn't see out, and I figured for twenty dollars I could sort of . . ."

Mr. Donald turned to Miss Nita, who was viciously whacking away at the woman in the next chair. "Did you *hear* that?" he cried. He held up a handful of Kate's hair again. "She trimmed it herself. With hedge clippers, apparently."

Miss Nita barely glanced at Kate before her attention was once again riveted upon her own perfect image in the mirror. She leaned lovingly into it and ran a moist finger over her Burnt Sienna lip gloss. "*Tell* me about it," she said.

Kate cowered under her salon smock, forced herself to take her eyes off Mr. Donald's glittering scissors, and saw Carol come out of the dressing room, wasp-waisted in her smock, flawlessly chic right down to the frosted toenails poking out of her espadrilles. Wasn't there another human

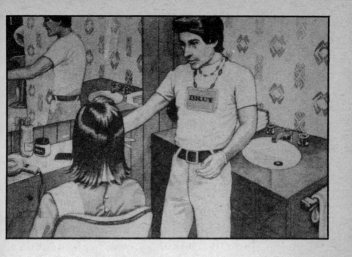

being in Marin, male, female or undecided, who fought a losing battle with Pepperidge Farm cookies? Who ought to lose ten pounds but couldn't stand calisthenics? Who'd tried jogging and bicycling but rapidly bummed out on watching her knees go up and down?

Sometimes Kate felt she was the only pocket of suburban blight left in Marin and that one of these days, someone was going to knock on her door with an environmental impact report in hand, give her ten minutes to pack her hedge clippers, and bundle her off to live in Daly City.

Nevertheless, she was pleased to see Carol and still more pleased when Carol spotted her and came over to kiss her on the cheek. Not only was Kate a little insecure these days, what with Harvey hardly making the scene at home at all and Paco urging her constantly to get out there and hustle up dogs, but her friends seemed to be avoiding her.

Angela Stein had stopped speaking to her weeks ago, even in group. Martha was distinctly cool when Kate phoned her at the motel where she and Bill and the kids were staying while the insurance adjusters had their house rebuilt. And even Julie, her old friend from Beginning Macramé, seemed to have written her off. Last time Kate phoned to ask her to lunch, because she really needed someone to confide in, Julie had said that she was "going through changes" these days and "not really up for lunches."

Paranoia, of course, was Harvey's bag, but Kate was starting to feel a little out of it. Were her friends trying to make a statement?

"So how's by you?" Carol said. "Listen, Donald here's a *genius*, isn't he. That's one terrific line he's giving you."

"You think so?" Kate asked nervously. "I guess he's doing the best he can. My hair's practically *screaming* for protein."

Over her shoulder, Carol revolved slowly in the mirror, checking herself out. "Well," she said, "you gotta work with what you've got, you know? Which reminds me. You still got Harvey?"

How and why did Carol always manage to

make Harvey sound like a very old car? "Of *course* I've still got Harvey," Kate said, bristling. With Mr. Donald making despairing little clucking noises at her, she felt she needed to make a statement herself. "I've also got a lover these days, as it happens. I mean, I thought it was time."

"You better believe it," Carol said. "I thought you were *never* gonna make it with anybody but your husband. Hey, who is it? Anybody I know?"

"I don't think so. He's this artist, sort of," Kate answered carefully. She still couldn't deal with the way people reacted when she told them Paco was just temporarily clipping dogs. "His name's Paco, and he's really terrific-looking, you know? Argentinian. From Argentina."

She saw Carol's eyes and Mr. Donald's lock in the mirror just as Mr. Donald's scissors nicked her right ear, drawing blood. "You're getting it on with *Paco?*" Carol asked incredulously. "Paco from El Perro?" To Kate's discomfiture, she grinned broadly. "Now, that's a mind-blower. *Really.* I mean, you and Donald have a lot in common, you know?

Mr. Donald was also grinning at Kate in the mirror, but there was something about the grin Kate found less than reassuring. "I *must* tell Paco," he said nastily, "that he's *got* to stop cutting your hair, Mrs. Holstein. Even if he does give you a discount." He nicked Kate's ear again. "It *ruins* the line.

"Tell me, sweetie, does Paco also clip your toenails? I have to hand it to him, Paco's *marvelous* on toenails."

"Holroyd," Kate said faintly. "It's not Holstein, it's Holroyd." She felt clammy beneath her smock, but the sight of blood always did that to her. Hadn't she passed out cold at *Bullitt* a couple of years ago?

Still grinning at Donald, Carol produced a Kleenex and dabbed at Kate's ear. "Kate," she said, "think of it this way. What's more important, some dude or a really terrific haircut? So Paco's gay. So he practically lives with Donald. You've still got good old Harvey . . . haven't you?"

32. Harvey tries to cope

Years ago, when the Holroyds first moved to Marin, wife-swapping was heavy-duty news in the *San Francisco Chronicle,* which described life in the suburbs, in sweaty prose, as one dizzying round of group interaction.

Apparently, though, as Harvey soon learned, he and Kate had moved to the wrong suburb. Sutton Manor went in for garage sales and an annual fair at the elementary school down the street where mothers sold homemade potholders and plants and fathers were expected to pick up the garbage.

So much for his erotic fantasies, mainly derived from *Behind the Green Door.* But now that he was living them with Ms. Murphy and company, Harvey found he'd just as soon pick up garbage. For total mental and physical exhaustion, nothing beat group sex except the decathlon.

Days at the bank, when he should have been working on his flow charts, Harvey prepared for the nightly revels, working out possible combinations on his Texas Instruments mini-calculator, with himself as the floating variable.

Nights at Ms. Murphy's Sausalito playpen, he mainly worried about his back. His spinal column was threatening to go AWOL, which, he was sure, wouldn't excuse him from duty. Ms. Murphy probably found wheelchairs a turn-on.

At least he was getting even with Kate and her lover, whom Harvey thought of as El Creepo, but to his chagrin Kate didn't seem to notice. When she was home at all these days, she trailed around the house in her Vanity Fair bathrobe, which smelled, to Harvey, faintly of dog, chain smoking and Martini & Rossi. Nor could he get her to dialogue with him beyond an inflectionless "Far out."

Then there were the practical problems, such as the one he confronted tonight. Somehow Harvey had to do his laundry, because he couldn't face another day with mismatched ankles, and that meant taking on the harvest gold Maytag, gleaming malevolently in the family room of his tract house.

Two o'clock in the morning found him confronting it and wondering when Maytag had merged with Lockheed. The dials on the washing machine looked like the instrument panel on a Concorde; Harvey couldn't decide whether to wash his socks or hijack the thing and fly it to Paris.

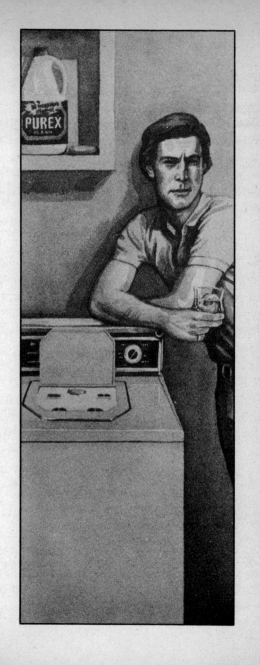

Kate used to do his laundry, of course, but Kate had apparently run through her wash cycle. What was convenient about a "marriage of convenience"? Harvey decided to think about it over a Cutty.

Joan found him rummaging in the refrigerator for ice, still clutching his reeking armful of socks, when she came back from a concert at the Cow Palace, deafened from the Doobie Brothers' amps. "Harvey," she shouted, coming up behind him, "why are you putting your socks in the freezer?"

Harvey dropped his laundry on the kitchen floor, sagged against the breakfast bar and waited for his pulse to return to dull normal. Why did Joan have to creep around the house at night like something out of *Helter Skelter?*

"Well," he said finally, "I'm making Sno-kones."

"Funny, Harv. Yuk. Yuk." Joan looked at him as if he were a dog turd, stepped stiffly around him and headed for the cupboard where Kate kept her stash of Pepperidge Farm Milanos. In her black satin Western shirt, her Frye boots and her skin-tight jeans, she reminded Harvey of *Midnight Cowboy*.

"Where the hell have *you* been?" he asked her.

Joan ignored him. Mouth full of cookie, she stared over his head. "Harv," she said, "could you move your socks? Like, out onto the patio or something? Because they smell outrageous. I mean, they're really grossing me out."

Harvey watched Joan scarfing down Milanos, biting them in half with her even teeth. Seventy bucks a month he'd paid for those teeth, to an orthodontist who spent his winters in the Bahamas.

"Listen," he said, "I can dig it. They're grossing me out, too, you know? So how about showing me how to run the Maytag, because I can't figure out how to start the water. I think it's because I'm a fire sign or something."

Joan destroyed another Milano. "No way, Harv. I'm not into that laundry bag."

"Joannie," Harvey said, "who loves ya, baby? Hey, I fixed your teeth, remember? I mean, I've done you a favor or two.... Wow, you looked like Jimmy Carter."

Joan crumpled the cookie bag and slammed the cupboard door.

"Harv," she snapped, "will you get *off* it?"

"No, really; you didn't even have a chin. No chin to speak of; it was just, like, vestigial. You woulda spent the rest of your life hauling logs in a beaver dam."

"Harvey," Joan said, "you're something *else*. You think I'm gonna wash your socks just because I *happen* to be a female person?"

"How about because I just paid the bill

on your charge account at Moody Blues? *Forty bucks* for one pair of jeans. What are they made out of, unborn denim?"

This time what Joan slammed was the hall door. Joan always slammed doors instead of closing them, so Harvey was prepared for the sonic boom. Had she at least jarred loose the ice trays?

She hadn't, so he resigned himself to lukewarm Cutty, started the water running and dumped his socks in the sink. No liquid detergent to be found, and he couldn't wash his socks with S.O.S. pads. No way of drying them once he got them washed because the dryer was just as inscrutable as the Maytag. "CAUTION," read a sticker on its door. "DO NOT OPERATE WITHOUT REMOVING LINT." From what, for God's sake? he wondered. His navel?

All Harvey wanted out of life at the moment was to pop his Sominex and catch a few z's before he had to face another awful dawn; but he had to do something about the tangle in the sink. Could you dry socks on a Salton Hotray? Divorce your wife for benign neglect?

Leaving his laundry to stew in its juices, he staggered down the hall to his Posturepedic. Tomorrow it was back to the bank, which was once his refuge but wasn't any longer. Not with Ms. Murphy an intercom away and nothing on her mind but giving him a buzz. . . .

33. Joan hits the road

Joan and Spenser were hanging out at Stinson, Joan having cut out of Tam High for the day while Spenser felt he needed "some rays on the bod." He also had to "see this dude about some stuff," he told Joan, who knew better than to ask a lot of questions. Spenser liked to keep a low profile.

Just now they were blasting "White Rabbit" halfway to Bolinas on Spenser's portable tape deck, finishing a six-pack and getting stoned. Spenser was also scanning the beach for park rangers because, he said, a narc in Smokey the Bear drag was still a narc.

Elementary street smarts, like Spenser's pet theory that narcs invariably wore brown shoes. "They get this discount at J. C. Penney's. Penney's is a CIA front," he explained.

Joan thought it was cool how Spenser was onto Penney's, but couldn't help worrying that he was paranoid. Yesterday they'd been hanging out downtown when this meter maid went by on her tricycle. Spenser had locked himself in the Chamber of Commerce rest room.

Right now, though, Spenser was mellow, so Joan was trying to tell him about her scene. "All we do in English is role-playing," she said. "So I asked him, What's all this role-playing jive. So *he* said ... Hey, you wanna know what he said?"

Spenser was wailing with Grace Slick.

"Listen, you wanna hear what *he* said?" Joan was beginning to get ticked off, because rapping with a guy whose life was one long toke wasn't her idea of a meaningful relationship. "He said role-playing was a prereq or something and I had to take it so I could take body language. . . . Hey, Spenser, are you *listening* to me?"

Spenser gave her his usual spacy smile. "Sure," he said vaguely. "You wanna hit?"

From the parking lot behind them came the voice of some dude with a van talking into his powerful CB. "Any ears out there? Any ears?" he was saying. "This is San Anselmo Slim, over and out. . . ."

"Far *out*," Spenser cried, subsiding into a fit of giggles.

Joan snapped the pop top on the last can of beer. "Spenser," she said, "pay attention. Okay? Because I'm trying to tell you, I'm totally bummed out. Kate's getting it on with this guy that clips these dogs, except she says how he's really an artist. And Harvey's weird. I mean, he's *always* weird, but he's getting weirder. You know where I found him the other night? Washing these dumb executive-length socks he wears and drinking Scotch. In the middle of the *night*. You know?"

Spenser was methodically scanning the beach. "I can't believe it," he said to Joan. "This place is practically *crawling* with narcs. See that guy with the inner tube?"

Joan gathered up her Famolares, her shoulder bag and Kate's tube of Bain de Soleil. "Spenser," she snapped, "are you gonna listen? I mean, can't you even *try* to relate?"

Spenser seemed to find this hilarious. "Any ears out there?" he mimicked. "Wow, I gotta get me a CB, you know? I'm gonna be a man in a van." He turned around and shouted toward the parking lot. "Hello, good buddy, this is the Fairfax Freak. . . ."

"Okay. That's it. I'm splitting, Spenser. I'm gonna hitch back up the mountain. Because I've *had* it with you, you know? Who do you think you are anyway, David Bowie?"

"Naw," Spenser said. "I'm just into role-playing. I just did David Bowie, right? Now watch. I'm gonna do Robert Redford."

Joan stomped off. When she looked back at Spenser from a distance, he'd fired up Grace Slick again and was sitting cross-legged, swaying gently back and forth and making rabbit ears.

Once she'd left Stinson, Joan arranged herself at the side of the road with one hip forward and her hair sort of casually over one eye. Kate and Harvey would have freaked if they knew she was hitching, but Joan figured she could take care of herself, having taken self-defense for PE last year because it beat yoga, her other choice. Kate studied yoga, and Kate was crazy. She thought her navel was the center of the universe.

When the VW bus stopped, she checked it out: man, woman, baby and this weird-looking dog, and they all looked mellow except for the dog. Joan climbed in with some difficulty, because she was still stoned out of her gourd, and by the time they'd made it to the top of Mount Tam, she'd agreed to drop out of the space she was in and go on with them to a commune in New Mexico.

Harvey answered the phone when she called the house several hours later from a truck stop where Jim was trying to fill his Thermos with Red Zinger tea and Rita was changing the baby, Chairman Mao. "Joan," he bellowed, "where the hell are you?"

When was Harvey going to learn she couldn't relate to being yelled at?

"I'm in L.A. or someplace. With Jim and Louise and Mao," Joan said. "It's cool, you know? Jim and Louise are sort of hanging out and I'm walking the wolf."

She waited for Harvey to subside. "The

wolf," she repeated, with infinite patience. "They've got this really terrific wolf. Listen, don't *worry* about it, okay? Wolves are far out; they just get a bum rap. I mean, this one's really a *pussycat*."

Kate was now on the other phone, making incoherent noises. "Hey," Joan said, as she had a sudden insight, "you ever notice the dial on a phone? Wow, it just hit me. It's this *mandala*. . . ." .

Harvey was telling her to come home immediately. Then he was telling her to stay where she was. "I'm gonna come and get you," he yelled. "Listen, Joan, did you hear what I said?"

"Sure," Joan said to him serenely. She put her free hand over her head and made rabbit ears. "I hear you, Harv. Over and out. . . ."

34. Bill gets involved

"I can't believe Kate," Martha said to Bill. "Her kid's split for Sandstone or someplace, her marriage is falling apart—even her damned dog's got pneumonia. That Latin type she was trucking around with clipped him right down to the knuckles, you know? And then it rained. . . ."

"Martha," Bill said, "I'm watching Walter Cronkite."

"So what do you think she's doing about it all? I mean, what do you think she's *doing* about it?"

"Writing a treatment for Norman Lear?"

"She's taken up *bargello*," Martha said. "Did you ever hear anything so freaky? She told Naomi how she makes these little stitches and it gives her this sense of order in the universe."

"Well," Bill said, "it beats burning down houses." He wished Martha wouldn't talk during Walter Cronkite, because Walter gave him a sense of order in the universe.

"*Anyway*, I'm really worried. I mean, needlework's fine, but it's not a *lifestyle*. Listen, could you turn off the tube?"

Bill reluctantly turned off the television

and sat back down on the motel bed. The one thing he dug about the Edgewater Inn, where he and Martha and the kids were staying, was that it got terrific reception. But Martha would never let him watch because she blamed the networks for Gregor's problem.

"You know he watched that two-hour special," she'd said to him shortly after the fire, "the one where the Waltons' house burned down. So the way I see it, he figured fires were okay if CBS showed one during the family hour."

Bill dug under the bed for the bourbon, which Martha discreetly hid from the chambermaid. "Listen," he said, "you watching Gregor?" This was Thursday, and according to the contract, Martha was in charge of the kids.

"I just checked him out," Martha reassured him. "It's cool. He's down the hall kicking the Coke machine."

"What about Tamalpa and Che?"

"Out throwing rocks in the swimming pool. Listen, I *mean* it; I'm worried about Kate. Don't you think we ought to do something?"

"Martha," Bill said, "you been up to the house today? How much longer do we have to stay here? And no, I don't think we ought to do something. What did you have in mind, calling up Sandstone?"

"I'm sure it's got an unlisted number.

They must get crank calls like crazy, you know? . . . About three weeks if it doesn't rain again. They still have to glue on the deck or something. . . . Anyway, what I *thought* was, you could talk to Harvey. Tell him how he's got to take responsibility."

"No way. I don't want any part of it. Leave me out of this, Martha, okay?"

"Wow, that's what's wrong with the *world*, you know? I mean, nobody wants to take responsibility. Don't you remember Kitty Genovese?"

Bill engaged Martha in hard eye contact. "Look," he said, "I'm telling you upfront. I didn't murder Kitty Genovese."

"No," Martha said, "but you didn't get *involved*."

Bill marveled again at the way Martha's mind worked, which never failed to blow him away. Martha was given to leaps of logic that made arguing with her like wading up to the hip in yogurt.

Now she was staring at him reproachfully. "Wow," she said again. "That poor girl. She could have screamed her head off, you know? And you would have kept right on watching *television*."

Gregor saved him from having to answer by crashing noisily into the room. "Martha," he shouted, "guess what I saw? I saw a accident out on the freeway."

"That's nice. sweetie," Martha said absently.

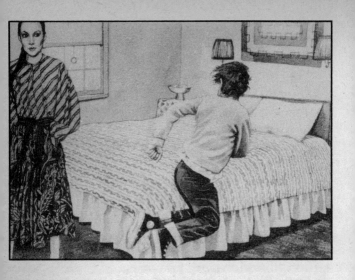

"Yeah," Gregor said. His eyes were shining. "The fuzz came, and they had sirens
and *everything*. I think a whole lotta people
got *hurt*."

Alarmed, Bill poured himself more bourbon. "Martha," he asked, "what does Steinmetz say? You take Gregor for a session
today? It freaks me how he gets off on rear-
enders. I don't think it's healthy, you
know?"

"Hey. That's a value judgment, sweetie. I
mean, *health* is just a word, okay? R. D.
Laing says society's sick and you've gotta be
insane if you're gonna be healthy. Like,
schizophrenics are *super*healthy; they've
really got their act together."

"Steinmetz go along with that?"

"Well, partly. He goes along with it *partly*. He says he's more of a Freudian, actually. He's trying to get Gregor in touch with his childhood." Martha neatly sidestepped Gregor, who was kicking her rhythmically in the ankle.

"For God's sake, Gregor's seven years old."

"I know. That's one thing he's got going for him. I mean, he can't have repressed *too* much. Listen, you keep changing the subject: what are you going to do about Harvey? Because somebody's got to get through to him, you know?

"Gregor, please stop acting out. Mommy's not a Coke machine. Coke machines are different from people; they don't have nerve endings like people do. . . ."

Bill beat Gregor to his bourbon glass. "Martha," he said, "will you knock it off? I'm gonna tell you what I'm getting. I'm getting you're trying to make me feel guilty."

"Well, *I'm* getting you feel guilty about Kate, because you know she must feel guilty about the house, so you're trying to make *me* feel guilty about making you feel guilty. But it's *your* life, right? So you're in charge of it. You feel guilty, that's *your* problem."

Bill had a feeling he was on a fast track. "Listen, Martha, I don't feel guilty. I didn't turn Kate on to bargello. I didn't even clip the goddamned dog."

"Of *course* you didn't," Martha said serenely. "Nobody said you did, so don't be so paranoid. But you've still gotta get involved, you know? Otherwise it's history, like, repeating itself. It's Kitty Genovese all over again."

Bill studied Martha with genuine admiration. Martha was one of a kind, a true original. Conceding defeat, he poured another drink. "Yeah," he said. "I see what you mean. . . ."

35. The need for commitment

Harvey agreed to meet Bill at Ethel's because Bill said on the phone that he had something heavy to lay on him and thought they ought to get together in a nurturing environment. Ethel's did a mind-blowing minted trout. Minted trout was nurturing. And evading Ms. Murphy for one evening, Harvey thought, might just be the saving of his sanity or at least his lower back.

He was a little spooked, though, because he didn't know where Bill was coming from, and so he fortified himself on a couple of Heineken's at the *no name* before he made the funk-and-fern scene at Ethel's. Beside him at the bar, an advertising type was coming on strong with a chick in the rich-peasant look, complete with the jewel-studded babushka Ms. Murphy had flipped over in Joseph Magnin's Christmas catalogue. "I want to get together some loving, seeking people so we can put together a really altruistic portfolio," he was saying earnestly.

On the other side, a woman he'd seen in the *no name* for years was talking to a Sausalito writer Harvey recognized, the one who'd had that best seller a few years ago about how he'd dropped out of the rat race and found happiness on a chicken ranch near Mount Shasta. Apparently the writer had moved back to the rat race on his royalties. "I think it's so *terrific*," the woman said, "how you're able to plug into yourself, and find this conduit into your unconscious, and be able to tap all that energy and keep flashing on it."

The writer preened, Harvey groaned. The *no name* was totally weird, totally façade, and he didn't know why he kept going back there, except that Marin bars were pretty much all into the same gestalt: imported beer, veggies and sour cream dip for hors d'oeuvres, and a clientele so laid back their collective energy level couldn't run an electric toothbrush.

At Ethel's he studied the menu, which took up the entire table, and waited for Bill, while the waiter squatted geisha-like beside him, describing the daily special. Ethel's waiters always squatted beside the tables, a touch Kate had always found terrifically *intime*. "The minted trout *is* fabulous," the waiter said, "but you might want to consider the special. If you're into taking risks."

Harvey greeted Bill with relief. "Hey, hey," he said, "how's the house coming along? You still living in the Edgewater or are you back in your own space?"

"Still in the Edgewater," Bill said,
sighing. "Listen, though, I don't blame Kate
anymore, okay? It was just sort of a gut reaction. I mean, I felt really bummed out about
the stuff we lost, and I had to blame somebody. You ever lose a mature *Ficus benjamina* that you'd raised from a six-inch
pot?"

"No," Harvey said. "I never did."

"Well, listen, it's a *trip*. I swear to God,
when I came up the hill that night and saw
all the smoke, I thought of it right away.
Like, I thought I could hear it screaming in
there and I just flipped out; they had to keep
me from going in."

"I can relate. I mean, I know how Kate
feels about her asparagus fern."

Bill unfolded his napkin and spread it on his lap, nearly winging the waiter, who had squatted cozily beside their table again. "Harv," he said, "that's what I want to talk to you about. Martha asked me to. But it's going to be hard to verbalize."

"You're supposed to talk to me about Kate's asparagus fern? Hey, look, let's order. We don't wanna keep this guy hunkering on his Adidas all night." He looked down into the waiter's eyes and ordered the minted trout.

"The veal on the special," Bill said. "I feel like taking risks. Carrot soup. A bottle of Muscadet. Salad *after*." The waiter unfolded and went away. "You have to tell them," Bill said to Harvey. "Even here. Otherwise they serve the salad before. Anyway, Martha thought you ought to know, Harv, although this is gonna be kind of hard to take." He leaned forward and lowered his voice. "Kate's into bargello."

"She's into Jell-O?"

"*Bargello*. It's needlework . . . little tiny stitches. Martha says Kate practically doesn't do anything else. She thinks it's totally compulsive behavior. I mean Joannie's gone, you're screwing around, Donald Barthelme's in intensive care at the vet's . . . what has Kate got left? *Bargello*, Harv. Is that your idea of a lifestyle?"

"Well," Harvey said uncomfortably, "maybe she's just burned out on macramé.

She used to groove on macramé. Maybe she's just going through changes needle-workwise."

"Harv, listen, I'm gonna be totally honest with you," Bill said, waving a spoonful of carrot soup. "You've gotta *commit* yourself, man, because if you're not committable, you're never gonna have a real commitment. And if you don't have a real commitment, what have you got? *Think* about it."

Harvey thought about it. He had Ms. Murphy, a bad back, another load of dirty laundry and a persistent fear that he was coming completely unglued. This morning at the bank, when he'd got a Coke out of the machine, he'd found himself staring at it, convinced the bottle was trying to tell him something: "No Deposit, No Return."

"Hey," he said, "you're *right*, you know? I mean, you are so totally right I can't believe it. Wow. Are you *right*."

Bill nodded, pleased, and put down his soup spoon. He dug in one of the pockets of his Levi's safari pants and brought out a small notebook. "I knew you'd see it that way," he said, "because you're incredibly open. Hey, listen, will you do me one? Will you sort of write me a note for Martha? Because she made me promise that I'd get through to you. I made this *commitment*." He flushed under Harvey's stare. "I mean, it's no big deal. . . ."

Harvey leaned closer to circumvent the

waiter, who was once again on his haunches beside the table, pepper grinder poised. "No way," he said. "That's *ridiculous*. I mean, I'm not gonna commit myself in *writing*, for God's sake."

"Harv," Bill said plaintively, "I wasn't exactly straight with you. I wasn't really open. I mean, I'm still at the Edgewater like I told you, but Martha's back at the house; so write me the note, okay? Because I keep thinking . . . maybe if I cut it back, I can still save the *Ficus*. But I've really gotta *move* on it, you know?"

36. Going through changes

Harvey wished Kate would put down her needlework and really zero in on what he was telling her, because something about her body language, as she sat in the Eames chair poking her needle in and out, reminded him of Madame Defarge knitting while the tumbrils rolled in the streets. He'd seen the flick as a kid in Spokane and now had a disturbing sense of *déjà vu*.

"What I *mean* is," he said, "I've been thinking about it, you know? And the way I figure, you've got to make a commitment. Because if you're not committable, you've never got a real commitment. And if you haven't got a real commitment, what have you got?"

"Heavy, Harv." Kate jabbed at her bargello. "Really heavy. Have you been reading Charles McCabe again? Wow, that's really *deep*."

"No, listen. I mean it, right upfront. You've gotta be committable. Because if you're not committable. . . ."

"You're committable, *really*," Kate said acidly. "So just relax. I mean, I could have you committed anytime. Angela Stein

thinks you're *psychotic*. And she's getting it on with a Ph.D. in behavioral psychology."

Advantage Kate; Harvey decided to try his backhand. "Yeah, well," he said, "it works both ways. I mean, who took up with a goddamn dog clipper? You still seeing El Sleazo these days? Hey, I coulda sued him for malpractice, you realize that? Alienation of affection and offing my dog."

Kate put down her needlework and rummaged in the pocket of her mama-san apron for a Kleenex. "That was a low blow, Harvey," she said. "You *know* how rotten I feel about Donald." She dabbed at her eyes. "Dr. Gelt says it's a profound trauma when you lose an only dog like that; he's written an article about it for a journal or something.

And he's going to start therapy sessions for the bereaved down at the pet hospital one of these days. He says there's this whole new field to explore, because when you have to castrate a male dog, for example, the male owner feels terrifically *threatened*. I mean, he's had these guys practically go into *hysterics* in the consultation room—isn't that fascinating? And then there's the whole bit about dog people and cat people. . . ."

"Kate," Harvey said, "get off it about dogs, okay? I don't wanna talk about dogs, I wanna talk about *human beings*. I mean, I wanna talk about *us*. . . . So Joannie's split. So Donald cashed in his chips. We've still sort of got each other, haven't we?"

He wished Kate wouldn't cry like that, because it made him feel completely devoid of socially redeeming importance and also because Kate never cried without dislodging at least one contact lens. Harvey hated crawling around on the wall-to-wall looking for contact lenses.

"Harvey," Kate said, making a determined effort to stay together, "I'm going to tell you what I think. I'm going to level with you, Harvey. I think marriage is a *living organism*. It's like an amoeba or something. What do you think happens to an amoeba when you take away practically its entire life-support system?"

"Well," Harvey said judiciously, "I expect it's a profound trauma. Especially if it's an only amoeba. I mean, is that what you mean?"

"*Exactamente*," Kate said. She still liked to use her Spanish, even with Paco having signed on as Mr. Donald's shampoo person and moved into his condo on Spyglass Hill, because despite everything, Paco had enriched her cultural heritage. "So you see, Harvey, I can't exactly get behind where you're coming from just because you've decided you're committable. Because being committable isn't the same as being committed. And anyway, this is *my* space, too. I'm the other half of the amoeba."

"Sure you are," Harvey said. "For *sure*. Like, I recognize that. Only what's the percentage, being half of an amoeba? Hey, whaddaya say we go for the whole shot? The whole living organism?"

Kate was staring at the M. C. Escher print over the fireplace. She'd picked up her needlework again, a gesture Harvey thought definitely hostile. The way he'd planned this whole scenario, Kate was supposed to fall into his arms, renew the commitment and then get busy washing his socks. Instead, he noticed unhappily, she had her "Uppity Women Unite" button pinned to the strap of her needlework bag and was looking at him, when she looked at him at all, with a decidedly clinical expression. The dentist looked at him like that when he was about to announce that Harvey needed another root canal job.

"Harvey," Kate said to him, "I've made this decision. I've decided I'm in charge of my own life, you know? So I've gotta take responsibility. I've gotta stop being acted *upon* and start acting. Do you know where I'm coming from?"

"Not exactly," Harvey said. "Another weekend brushup at est?"

"*Cheap shot,* Harvey." Kate stuffed her bargello into the bag and rose, with some difficulty, from the Eames chair, which she'd given him for Christmas some years ago when he'd asked for a Barcalounger. "Anyway, est is fantastic, no matter how you try to bad-mouth Werner. It teaches you how to permit yourself to *be*. Which is just what I'm gonna do; I'm gonna be *myself*. I'm gonna love myself. I'm gonna *accept* myself. Can you relate to that? Can you even begin to grasp the space I'm in?"

"Southwest corner of the living room," Harvey said, "about twenty-five feet above sea level. You want me to check out the longitude and latitude?" Something told him he'd written the wrong scenario and that Kate wasn't going to pick up his option. Would she at least fire Ms. Murphy and do a load of laundry before she got into just *being* full time?

"I'm moving out," Kate said. "I'm splitting. This weekend. I've found another environment, with loving, caring people. A whole different space. A warm, loving, caring, *committed* environment, Harvey, where I can be myself, my really authentic self."

Harvey asked the first panicky question that came to mind? "You're not taking the Maytag, are you? Listen, I'm really gonna need the Maytag."

"Only my clothes," Kate said serenely, "and Joannie's baby pictures and the Cuisinart. Oh, and 'Julia 2' and the asparagus fern. That's it. *Totalmente.*" She picked up her needlework bag and threw it at him. "I don't need this anymore. I'm breaking the need cycle. Give it a chance; you're gonna *love* bargello. . . ."

37. Kate's new space

Harvey didn't make the scene at home at all the Friday night before Kate moved out, so she left a note propped against the Salton peanut butter maker giving him her address and reminding him to feed Kat Vonnegut, Jr., who, she said, was "into Meow Mix."

It rather got to her to split without seeing Harvey at all, but maybe it was better this way, because his absence meant they could avoid charges and countercharges, the whole accusation-and-guilt syndrome that had plagued the marriage from the beginning.

Who was responsible for the communications breakdown? Which of them really was off on his own trip and unable to relate? Who was afraid to be open and honest about feelings, and which habitually forgot to line the garbage can with a Glad bag, so that they didn't indulge in elitist exploitation of the garbage men?

Kate didn't have the answers, except for the bit about the garbage, although she did feel that Harvey was practically a casebook study of a depressive personality acting out through anger. As she told her women's group, she really felt sorry for him because he had so little insight into his real motivations. But she couldn't stay in the same space with a manic-depressive, even when Harvey was in one of his "up" cycles, because, as the group had pointed out repeatedly, to do so was equivalent to being a professional victim who went around wearing a psychic "Kick Me" button. Furthermore, she was tired of Harvey's screwing around.

Given the dynamics of their interface, then, she had to make her move. And even as she fought back tears at the prospect of leaving her Stine graphics, her copper sauté pans, her Billie Holiday records and her Design Research modular seating components—all the painstakingly selected elements of the good life she and Harvey had once set out to share—Kate felt liberated. In political terms—and marriage was an exercise in power politics—she was freeing herself from the oppressor, shaking off her chains.

"Chains" reminded her that she hadn't cleaned out her jewelry box; she went back to the bedroom and got the stuff, stuffing it into a Pucci print bag that had come with a ten-dollar cosmetics purchase at Macy's. Finally, she dropped her house keys into the mailbox, piled her boxes and suitcases into the bus, and set off for Blithedale Canyon and her new, fully actualized life.

Kate had found her new pad through an ad on the bulletin board at the Golden Valley Market, offering a room in a communal living situation to "a mature, mellow female vegetarian into meditation, creativity and shared responsibilities. est graduate preferred." The address proved to be a rambling redwood house up several flights of stone stairs, just the Old San Francisco summer-vacation cottage she and Harvey had wanted to buy when they moved to Mill Valley. Complete with soaring ceilings and sagging decks, the house, as Kate told Martha, was "simply *screaming* with tranquillity." And while her own room proved to be a converted closet, Kate felt immediately in tune with its mellow atmosphere and its other residents.

Brian, who'd interviewed her to see whether she was astrologically compatible with the present occupants, was a landscape architect who free-lanced as a handyperson while he waited for the drought to end so that people could get back to the soil again. Gentle, nonaggressive and stoned out of his mind, he'd struck Kate as slightly off balance yin-and-yangwise but definitely benign. "The whole number here," he told her, "is giving each other space." He'd then shown her the closet.

Harold, who had a Ph.D. in sociology but was currently working as a stock clerk at Alpha Beta until something better shook down, struck her as an incredible intellectual heavy; she also sensed this terrific empathy from him right away. "So you're breaking out of the conventional, societally conditioned role models for women," he said approvingly. "*Far out.*" Kate noticed that Harold wore a sterling silver biological equality symbol over his tattered T-shirt; as she told him, it gave her positive vibes.

Woman, who'd changed her name legally from Debbie Ann Sulzberger, was a radical feminist who gave demonstrations in gynecological self-examination and collected money for free speculums for sisters at the bottom of the poverty ladder. Having satisfied herself that Kate had read Shulamith Firestone, Woman welcomed her warmly. "I was sort of hoping for a Third World person," she said, "but it hit me, that woulda been tokenism. Listen, you know anybody with a mimeograph machine?"

Gunther spoke very little English, was in his mid-fifties and ran a small appliance-repair service down in town. "He kind of came with the house," Brian explained to Kate, after Gunther had grunted a greeting at her and disappeared. "The woman who owns the place moved to the Sunset, so Gunther collects the rent and fixes stuff. He's an okay dude, but he's sort of *Germanic* about the money. Isn't into barter and won't take food stamps."

"It's cool," Kate said. "I've got the first and

last and the cleaning deposit. And I'm planning to really get down and grind out the macramé." She decided to be open and trusting. "I'm also sort of planning to do some writing," she said. Although living with Harvey had stifled her creativity terrifically, Kate had always felt that macramé was only a substitute for her real gifts of expression. She still had a novel in mind, loosely autobiographical though really about the universal female experience, but had so far only mentally designed the book jacket.

Brian was incredibly receptive. "Hey," he said, "you're a writer. So am I. I read my poetry down at the Book Depot on Wednesday nights, and the feedback's been *unbelievable*. You know anybody with a mimeograph machine?"

The fifth member of the household was Millie, who was eighty-five years old, a lifelong Sierra Club member and indefatigable hiker and, Woman told Kate privately, "a little wiggy. Don't leave anything valuable lying around, like your stash. She's one heavy old lady, and we let her move in because we wanted to make a statement about ageism in America, but she's got these sticky fingers. I'm sure she took my copy of *Against Our Will*, but I can't confront her about it without making waves."

Kate pulled up to the foot of the stone stairs this sunny Saturday morning a week later and looked up at the decrepit house in a happy glow of anticipation. Her first commune . . . and this evening the first house meeting with Kate as a member of her new extended family. Not to acquaint her with the rules, of course, because there weren't any. Just to give her some *guidelines.* . . .

38. Meaningful interaction in a commune

Only Brian was at the house when Kate moved in that Saturday afternoon. He didn't help her carry her bags and boxes up the stone stairs because to do so would have been a sexist put-down of women and their separate but equal muscle structure, but did show Kate her shelves in the communal refrigerator and the kitchen cupboard. "Remember," he reminded her, "no meat. Harold just smells it and he goes into anaphylactic shock."

Kate promised, though she'd never been a total vegetarian before except for a few weeks years ago when she'd gone macrobiotic and started hallucinating. Still, it was going to be good for her to maintain on veggies and clean all the yecch out of her system for once.

Anyway, the whole number about living with other people, which Harvey had never been flexible enough to grasp, was flexibility Kate prided herself on hers so didn't call upon her assertiveness training when her one-third of a vegetable bin proved full of somebody else's mung beans. Nor did she complain about her limited space in the converted closet that was her bedroom, though it reminded her of the elevator in the Russ Building. Claustrophobia was all in the mind.

True, she began to hyperventilate once the door was closed behind her. True, she had to walk across the bed to get to the rope slung across one corner on which she hung her Above the Crowd pant suit, her Saks caftans and her new menswear-look tuxedo from Modern Eve. These, however, were only minor inconveniences around the parameters of the total infrastructure. As Jerry Brown kept telling the Harveys of this world, you had to lower your expectations, and Kate was already lowering hers. She'd simply have to remember to put her head between her knees when she was suffering most acutely from the mind/body split and thought she was going to stop breathing entirely.

Then, too, she had the run of the entire rambling house, although Brian was sunbathing naked on the deck, Millie brought the whole Sierra Club "B" group back to the house for Gatorade after a hike while Kate was unpacking, and Woman soon surfaced with a group of sisters organizing a protest. "We're gonna picket chauvinist pig doctors who drape female patients in the examining room," she told Kate, unrolling shelf paper across the living room floor and passing out poster paints. "I mean, what the hell are we, persons or orifices?"

Kate said she thought women were definitely persons. "Damn right," Woman said. "So why do they make us wear those goddamn shower curtains?"

Next Gunther came to her door to collect her eighty dollars for the first month and forty more for a cleaning deposit, though as far as Kate could tell just eyeballing it, the house was longer on deposits than on cleaning. As she discovered when she ventured into the sun porch in her Bernardo barefoot sandals, Millie had a very old, half-blind tomcat that missed its litter box much of the time.

"Never mind, dear," Millie said to Kate, when she came upon her scraping her shoes, "it's only soybeans and a little miso. John Muir is a vegetarian."

Harold came home from Alpha Beta while Kate was putting away her kitchen stuff and her supply of brown rice, lentils and whole bran bought in bulk at the Co-op health food store. "*Fan*tastic," he cried, when he flashed on her Cuisinart. "Hey, can I take it for a spin around the block?" Kate consented graciously, though she felt that borrowing a person's Cuisinart was like borrowing her toothbrush or maybe even her diaphragm. Nervously, she watched Harold feeding tofu into the orifice; wasn't he giving it too much wrist? She went back

to her room, because she was getting up-tight, and for lack of anything else to do, walked around on her bed.

Finally, unsure of the game plan for who used the kitchen when, she got into her bus, went out to the freeway and ducked into McDonald's for a Quarter Pounder. No real options, she thought in her own defense, because nobody'd opened a fast-food lentil outlet in Mill Valley yet, though someone was bound to.

The house meeting was already in progress when she came back up the stairs, hoping that she didn't smell of Quarter Pounder and thus trigger one of Harold's allergy reactions, which, Brian said, were "something *else*." "Listen," Brian was saying fiercely to Harold as they faced off across the golden oak coffee table, "you gotta wash your dishes, you dig? Because I get to cook after you get to cook, and you never wash your lousy dishes. In *addition* to which, you've been eating my granola. Why can't you get your *own* crunchy granola?"

"You ate my mozzarella," Harold snapped. "Why can't you get your own mozzarella? Anyway, I don't get off on dishes. You want the dishes washed, that's *your* priority."

Kate took a seat in a battered wicker chair. She smiled at everyone to show she was neutral, sort of like Switzerland, pulled out her Bic and lit a cigarette.

Millie began to flap her arms violently. "*Do* you mind? I'm not into cigarette smoke."

Woman agreed with Brian that Harold was Superslob. "You stir-fry stuff in that goddamn wok and you leave this oil slick forty miles wide. Who do you think you are, Standard Oil of California?"

Harold said he didn't stir-fry, he *chowed*. Furthermore he chowed in cold-pressed safflower oil. He also said Chinese cooking was an art form and then complained to Kate about her Cuisinart. "It *creamed* my tofu," he said belligerently. "Like I didn't want it totally *destroyed*."

Kate said she had "this thing" about her Cuisinart and wished Harold wouldn't put tofu in it. She added that she never could get behind tofu and figured her Cuisinart was on the same wavelength.

Gunther had been sitting quietly in a corner but suddenly decided to join in the dialogue; red-faced, he charged Woman with losing his Phillips screwdriver. Woman said Gunther was macho tripping and explained that it *really* meant that he was worried about his tool.

Millie said she wished Woman wouldn't talk dirty.

Several hours later they were still interacting, with Kate participating in the group dynamic. "It's not the mung beans," she told Harold heatedly, when she'd learned who'd preempted her share of the vegetable bin. "The *point* is I've gotta have a place for greenies. I mean, I can't keep going to McDonald's every night."

Right away Harold's pupils disappeared and he began to turn the muted gray of a Quarter Pounder. Kate watched the sweat break out on his forehead, horrified at her insensitivity. "Oh, wow, I'm *sorry*," she said contritely. "Maybe I oughtà just go in and crash. . . ."

Back in the closet, she fired up a cigarette, resisting the impulse to chew up and swallow it. Was this what Virginia had in mind when she wrote about "a room of one's own"?

39. Life imitates art

"It's cool," Harvey said to Jerry from the car
pool, over a beer at the Sausalito Food
Company. "I'm picking up the pieces. But it
was pretty rough right after Kate split. For
one thing, Kat Vonnegut, Jr., got really
weird and went on this hunger strike or
something. I had to hold him down for a
while there and pour milk down his throat
with the bulb baster."

"Well," Jerry said, "it figures, Harv. Cats
can't verbalize their feelings."

Harvey inspected the scratches on his
wrists. The crystal on his Pulsar looked like
a road map. "*Really*. Anyway, he's coming
around. He's pretty together again these
days, although he seems to need constant
stroking."

Jerry made eye contact as best he could
through the bottom halves of his gradient
lenses. "If you get my meaning," he said
carefully, "he may have been sort of picking
up vibes. I mean, you haven't been too
together yourself."

"I've been together. I've been *totally*
together."

Jerry smiled and nodded knowingly.

"Sure, you've been *together*, Harv, but in this really fragmented way. Like I said to Jody right after the split, 'Harvey's really hurting, you know? He's trying to finesse it, but he's really hurting.'"

Harvey swallowed the rest of his beer, untangled himself from an overhead grape ivy and conspicuously consulted his Pulsar. "Hey," Jerry said, "who mugged your watch?"

"Look, I've gotta be moving on. I've got somebody waiting for me." Harvey winced as Jerry grinned and punched him solidly in the arm.

"Far out," Jerry said. "I hope this is the biggie, Harv. Because I've always had this insight about you. You wanna know what I said to Jody?"

Harvey decided having a drink with Jerry, on a scale of 1 to 10, was a decimal point above coming down with swine flu.

"'Emotional intimacy is not his number.' That's what I said to Jody, and *she* said, wow, I really had a line on you."

Harvey headed for his bike, thinking that he also had a line on Jerry and an insight that Jerry had incredibly bad breath. He should have made a citizen's arrest; breath like that belonged on a chicken hawk.

On the way out he passed their waitress, who'd earlier refused to give him her phone number because, she'd explained, she was already committed. "It's really a beautiful

relationship, and he's really a beautiful person, but I've only known him twenty-four hours. I'm just hoping everything stays copacetic."

Harvey gave her a jaunty wave. He wanted her to know that he had a lot of ego strength and didn't take rejection as a sign of rejection.

Outside the Food Company he checked out the chain lock that secured his Motobecane against ripoff artists and then walked down to the end of Gate 5 road to look at the sailboats in the yacht harbor. Maybe he could sign on to crew for somebody headed for the Bermuda Triangle, for how else could he pry loose Stella? Stella was driving him up the wall.

Before he'd gone to bed with her, Ms. Murphy had occasionally got out one rather grubby letter a day. Now he was lucky if she turned out an envelope, and the only place Harvey could get any work done, safe from his total squirrel of a secretary, was behind a locked door in the executive men's room.

He'd spent much of the afternoon there, his flow charts spread around his feet, but eventually Stella smoked him out. "Harv," she called languorously over the transom, "you gonna make the scene tonight or not? Because I thought I'd get on the horn and line up a few people."

"No lines," Harvey said wearily. "Not unless everyone takes a number. Look, how about we just go to a movie tonight for a change?"

Ms. Murphy pondered. "You mean, *first?*" she asked.

Harvey reluctantly abandoned the men's room. "You got that letter done?" he asked aggressively. "I mean, I don't wanna *rush* you, but it's been three hours. Like, Lincoln wrote the Gettysburg Address in three hours."

"Yeah, I know," Ms. Murphy said, running a finger down the front of his shirt. "I've always liked the part about 'four score.' Hey, you want your neck rubbed, Harv? You sound kinda uptight."

"I don't want my neck rubbed, I want my

letter typed. You know, Stella . . . 'up-typed'?"

Ms. Murphy undulated across the office as smoothly as a rotary-engine Mazda. "Later, Harv," she purred over her shoulder. "I'm a lover, not a typer."

Now he was due at the nightly orgy, a low-budget porno-maker's fantasy fit for the Emeryville underground film festival. Harvey mentally ran through the reel: 35mm. and a hand-held camera, with the denouement his back going out.

He couldn't face it, and once on his bike, headed for his place instead of Ms. Murphy's. Maybe he and Kat Vonnegut, Jr., could spend the evening watching Monday-night football, unless the Manx got a better offer.

Harvey made a pit stop at 7-11, thinking he'd take home a Hungry Man dinner, but they wouldn't let him bring his bike inside and he wasn't about to take his hands off it when there was nothing to chain it to except a large tree. No problem for a bike ripper-offer; they traveled these days with McCulloch chain saws.

He rode on to McDonald's, where he breakfasted every morning on Egg McMuffin, and wrapped himself around a Big Mac instead. At least Kate wouldn't be caught dead at McDonald's, and neither would anyone else he knew. Being a junk-food junkie, in Harvey's circle, was just this side of being a Keane collector.

Despite his back, he was really wailin' when he hung a sharp right into his driveway, pretending Sutton Manor was a picturesque village along the route of the Tour de France, and so didn't see Kat Vonnegut, Jr., until it was too late. Kat took a direct hit and turned in his lunch pail before Harvey could even get off his bike.

Why hadn't it rained tonight or something, so that he would have had to car-pool with Jerry, bad news, bad vibes, bad breath and all? Harvey regarded his ex-cat with tears in his eyes. *Slaughterhouse-Five* in his own damned driveway, and now he was alone for real. Kat Vonnegut, Jr., his good buddy, looked like something the cat dragged in. . . .

40. Gnats in the yogurt

Kate was discovering that what Harold called "a viable alternative to the family unit" was what Harvey called "a whole new ball game." Communal living was a mixed bag, no matter how you sliced it.

On the one hand, she'd liberated herself from Harvey, the family unit and the prior social conditioning that had kept her from being fully human. On the other, Brian used all the hot water, Millie stole things and Woman refused to clean up after herself in the kitchen because she'd "*had it* with that whole chauvinist Janitor in a Drum mentality." Woman said if God had meant women to clean kitchens, he would have given them S.O.S. pads instead of hands.

Kate, who confessed to being a neatnik, also found Harold a total slob and bitterly resented having to dispose of his crusted rice and congealed chow yuk before she could cook her own Veg-All patties. When she berated him he called her a racist and gave her a lecture on Chinese culture. Kate went back to scrubbing his pots for fear he'd plaster the house with wall posters, but told

Woman privately that Harold was "just *incredibly* psychotic."

Woman said men were all psychotic. She then turned around and took a swipe at Kate. "I wish you'd stop shaving your goddamn legs. You might not know it, but you're making a *statement*. Like, what have you got against the female body? Shaving your legs is decadent."

Kate said she'd never thought of it that way and promised Woman she'd stop being decadent. She didn't tell her that not shaving her legs made her miserably self-conscious, nor that in the event of nuclear holocaust, the first thing she'd grab was her Revlon eye-liner. Some prior social conditioning died hard.

These, however, were gnats in the yogurt, minor annoyances Kate could have swung with had it not been for her other, more oppressive problems. Although she'd begun work on her novel, she hadn't made significant progress; she kept sharpening pencils and then going blank. Brian said she was "trying too hard" and that when he suffered from writer's block, he got stoned out of his mind and "let it flow."

He said he'd written some dynamite poems that way and generously offered Kate part of a Thai stick, but nothing happened when she tried it except that she dropped her sharpened pencil and no way could she lower herself sixty feet to the floor to retrieve it. Later, she got sick to her stomach and threw up her soybean casserole.

Even her macramé was going badly, and Kate had counted on it to earn her a right livelihood. Somehow she kept turning out lopsided plant hangers she couldn't unload at the flea market even when she threw in the coleus slips she'd started in Veg-All cans. Gunther, meanwhile, was being Teutonic and leaning on her for the rent, flatly resistant to Kate's suggestion that he let her substitute an energy exchange. Gunther didn't believe in barter and wasn't into macramé. He also reacted with alarm when Kate offered to teach him raja yoga.

"Gunther," Kate asked, "don't you believe in body personality awareness?"

Gunther said he believed in money. He refused Kate's asparagus fern, her authentic Hopi turquoise necklace and finally her Cuisinart. Kate had to part with her remaining cash, wondering where her next eyeliner was coming from. At least she still had her charge accounts, though Macy's didn't sell macramé string; Kate figured Harvey owed her *that* much in back pay and workperson's comp alone.

At least Brian was *simpático,* even if Brian used her hair dryer and left a ring around the bathtub. Brian read her his epic poem "Labia," misted her fern when he misted his spider plants, and once even offered her a glass of Grower's while she scraped the grunge out of Harold's wok. Kate found herself confiding to him the multiple horrors of her marriage.

"I wanted an open, loving relationship, based on growth and trust and sharing, and Harvey wanted his Jockey shorts ironed. I mean, we just weren't coming from the same place at *all.*"

Brian said seriously that Harvey sounded like great material for primal therapy. "I'm into primaling myself, and it's really getting my head together. Like, it took me weeks of screaming myself hoarse, but I'm finally learning to reach through my defenses."

Kate was impressed. "That sounds *fantastic.* Hey, who are you screaming *with,* the Center for Feeling Therapy?"

Brian looked a little offended. "I'm not screaming *with* anybody," he said. "I'm just sort of . . . you know, *screaming.*"

Brian was also deeply into body personality awareness and spent long hours doing Tai chi on the deck. Kate loved to watch him rippling through the Monkey, his suntanned pectorals gleaming, and caught herself one afternoon wishing Brian weren't so young. Getting it on with younger men was definitely *in* these days, but despite Gestalt, est and Arica, Kate was still the victim of an outmoded Puritan ethic. Additionally, she worried about her bod,

having noticed recently she was so out of
shape, her thighs tended to follow her up
the stairs.

During a Tuesday-morning massage at
Moment's Pause, after which she intended
to jog all the way across the parking lot to
her bus, Kate wondered how she could ask
Brian obliquely whether or not he got off on
flab. Harvey, after all, still missed garter
belts and kept a Frederick's of Hollywood
catalogue squirreled away in his bicycle
bag.

Back at the house she went back to her
novel, determined, this time, to let it flow.
Soon, though, she pushed her yellow legal
pad aside and returned to aimlessly sharpening pencils. Apparently her life with

Harvey was just too *painful* to be confronted and transformed into enduring art. She'd simply have to wait until the healing process took over and she could remember where to put the commas again.

Depressed, she went in search of Brian. Maybe he'd like to help her tie macramé knots.

Brian, though, was otherwise engaged. Kate found him bare-chested in the bathroom, raptly turning a round brush in the hair of a chick who looked about thirteen and a half. "Hi, there," the girl said to Kate serenely, when she saw her standing in the doorway. "I guess I'm using your hair dryer, huh? Listen, I didn't bring a *thing*. You happen to have a Revlon eye-liner?"

41. Different strokes for different folks

"Welcome wagon," Martha called faintly, the morning she came to visit Kate. She sagged, winded, against the doorframe. "Wow, those stairs are *too much*. I keep telling myself I've gotta stop smoking."

Kate glanced nervously over her shoulder. "Don't light up around here," she said. "Millie freaks like you wouldn't believe. Like, last night I was smoking in my room, and she came bombing through the door with this Wizard air freshener.... Hey, isn't it *unbelievable* how some people still relate to aerosols? I mean, when you *think* about the ozone layer."

Martha was glad that she hadn't presented Kate with the housewarming present she'd brought her, a can of Black Flag for the scorpions. "*Really*," she said. "Live and let live."

Kate couldn't wait to give her the tour. "You know, when I found this place, I just *literally* fell over dead. I mean, I *literally* had a heart attack. They don't build houses like this anymore."

Martha looked at the sagging sun porch, crawling with Brian's spider plants. She also took in the rotting floors; one false move and you'd find yourself in the Mill Valley Market, down below, laid out among the Belgian endive, the walnut oil and the smoked salmon.

Kate had already gone springing off in her ripple-sole Famolares. Martha followed dutifully and planted a foot in something soft. "Hey," she said, when she'd inspected her shoe, "is this what I think it is?"

"Wow, I'm *sorry*. I should have warned you. Millie's got this terrifically old cat. Listen, though, it's only soybeans. He isn't on that carnivore trip."

Kate showed Martha the leaded-glass windows, the claw-footed tub and the blackened fireplace, large enough to smoke a salmon. "Is this funky, or is this *funky?*"

Martha thought it was more like scuzzy, but did like one of the house's amenities, Brian sunbathing on the deck naked except for his elephant hair bracelet. "Who's the centerfold?" she asked.

She thought she noticed Kate's neck reddening. "Oh," Kate said, "that's only Brian. Brian's heavily into the perfect tan. Hey, I wanna show you my room. I'm covering the walls with styrofoam egg cartons and then I'm gonna burlap over them. You know, for texture?"

Millie went scuttling out of Kate's door as she and Martha came down the hall. Kate thought she saw her stuffing something down the front of her chenille bathrobe. "Damn it," she snapped, "Millie's getting into my stuff again. Last week I caught her trying on my tux over that weird Gerald Ford cardigan sweater she wears, and you know what she *said* to me? She said I seemed to have this identity problem, and Stanford had this sex-change clinic. . . ."

"So?" Martha said. "You're overreacting. Listen, don't you know that anger is just the flip side of depression? It's just, like, the *symptom,* not the disease."

Kate picked at her Cost Plus madras bedspread. "I don't happen to be *diseased,*" she said huffily. "Maybe a little *warped* after living with Harvey and doing that earth mother bit for years." Tears began to run down the sides of her nose. "I mean, have *you* ever been Girl Scout cookie captain for three years in a row, because nobody else would take responsibility? Have *you* ever spent your whole life, practically, trucking around in the Red Cart Market listening to that awful canned music? 'Light My Fire,' by Mantovani. Have *you* ever lived across from a grade school and spent whole days scraping peanut butter sandwiches out of your goddamn juniper bushes?" She clutched Martha's hand so hard it hurt. "Listen, I'm *allergic* to juniper. It makes me hyperventilate."

Martha stared at Kate aghast, wondering if she should call the Crisis Center. "Hey,"

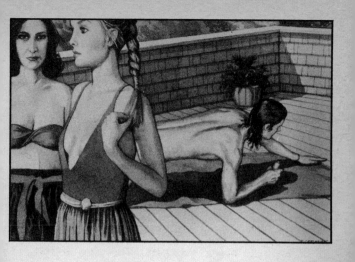

she said, "stay mellow, okay?" She thought it was time for touch therapy and put her arm around Kate's shoulder. "Listen, why don't we get out of here? The room's fantastic, and I *love* the egg cartons, but it's sort of a little small, you know?"

Kate sobbed loudly for another minute, took hold of herself and blew her nose. "Martha," she said, "what am I going to *do?* I mean, like for the rest of my life. Where am I going to *go*, Martha?"

Martha had a marvelous idea. "How about checking out the deck?"

Brian rolled over sinuously when Kate and Martha made the scene, presenting a suntanned bottom that looked like a whole-wheat Parker House roll. "You mind?"

Martha said to him. "We'd thought we'd get a little ozone."

"Outasight," Brian answered. "Just don't get between me and the rays, though. I'm working on the soles of my feet. Hey, Kate, how about doing my back?"

He reached for his bottle of Johnson's baby oil, but Kate lunged for it and got there first. Apparently she didn't want Brian to sit up.

Martha watched her gingerly oiling Brian's shoulder blade. She noticed that Kate's neck was flashing on and off. "Well," she said, "I think I'll split. We've gotta go to a gallery opening. Heavy-duty erotic art; Bill practically got off on the invitation."

Kate insisted on walking her out. "Martha," she said again, breathing audibly, "what am I going to *do? Really?*"

Martha slid out of her slippery grasp. "The other shoulder blade, for starters. And listen, kid, you've made the right move. I mean, wow. You've made the right move *totally.*"

Down in Mill Valley she headed for a pay phone, dug for a dime and called the tract house. "Harv," she said sweetly, "this is Martha. I just thought I'd ask what's coming down."

Harvey said the whole damned house was coming down and that at the moment he was bailing out the family room with the copper bowl Kate used for egg whites. He said the Maytag had gone bananas.

"What a bummer," Martha said. "I really feel for you, you know? I wanted you to know, though, I just saw Kate. She's really getting her act together; and listen, you're gonna just *love* Brian. I want to get you all over for dinner soon."

She stayed burned at Harvey all the way home. Talk about your double standard. . . .

42. Coming to terms with the external culture

Martha happily took in the vibes at the gallery opening in the Art and Garden Center. Thank God, Gregor, Tamalpa and Che were off to summer camp for a few weeks so she and Bill could make the Marin scene again.

"Isn't this totally *outrageous?*" she said to her neighbor Naomi Maginnis. She was glad she'd tucked her pants into her gaucho boots and worn her favorite Peruvian peasant blouse. Now that ethnic chic was in, nothing looked tireder than a JAG denim wrap skirt.

Naomi nodded. "*Really,*" she said. "Hey, isn't that Francis Ford Coppola? I thought he was still in the Philippines."

"Oh, yeah. Filming *Patton* or something." Martha followed Naomi's gaze and zeroed in on a woman in a corset top over several layers of ruffled taffeta skirt. "You oughta wear your glasses," she said. "That's the waitress from the Belly Deli, the one that's in my tap-dancing class. Anyway, Francis Ford's got a beard. And I don't think he tap-dances . . . that's Hayakawa."

Sipping wine out of plastic glasses, the

two of them contemplated the nearest painting, a gaping vagina in shocking pink acrylic. "Listen, Martha," Naomi demanded, "how do you feel about that, *really?*"

Martha wished she'd come by herself. "I dunno. How do *you* feel about it?"

Naomi knew a lot about art, while Martha herself had failed Art Appreciation. All she remembered from her dim college days were the names of a few no longer relevant heavies, and that to get purple, you mixed red and blue.

Naomi stepped back and squinted at the painting. "Well," she said, "the *plasticity's* amazing. Don't you think the plasticity's amazing?"

"I flashed on that right away," Martha said.

"And I also groove on the way she's concealed that almost *geometric* precision under what looks, when you just eyeball it, like purely random composition. That blob in the right-hand corner's sheer genius. I mean, it *defines* the entire conceptualization."

Martha felt hopelessly outclassed. "Isn't that the price sticker?"

Naomi sighed. "Ostensibly, yes. But you've got to go beyond surfaces, Martha. You've gotta relate to the manipulation of space."

Martha stepped closer and looked at the blob, a small red sticker with "$1200" on it.

"I guess I just don't know much about art. In the *technical* sense," she added defensively. "I just go by my gut reaction. Either I like it or I don't."

"So do you like it or don't you like it?" Looking pushed out of shape for some reason, Naomi rummaged in her purse. She put on her glasses with the Christian Dior frames.

"Well," Martha said, when she had to say something, "I sort of like it. I *kind of* like it. I mean, I do and I don't, you know?"

Under the guise of going for more popcorn, she set out through the crowd, looking for Bill. Fragments of conversation reached her: ". . . marvelously asexual eroticism; it turns you on and off simultaneously"; ". . . love that shocking pink she uses; it pulls you right *in*, you know where I'm coming from?": "... symbolism's really heavy; did you flash on how all of her phalluses have these terrific mushroom clouds on top?"

When she found him, Bill was engrossed in a painting that looked to Martha, just eye-balling it, interchangeable with the one Naomi had just explained to her. "Isn't that blob in the corner terrific? Like, it just *defines* the entire conceptualization."

Naomi's husband Jason stared at her. "Martha," he said acidly, "that's the price sticker."

Martha felt more in her element back in her kitchen making coffee, while Naomi kept her company and Bill and Jason played backgammon. "Wait till you taste Melior," she said. "You won't be able to get behind Chemex anymore. Anyway, I was telling you how Harvey came on when I called him this morning. After all that screwing around he's been doing, don't you think he could *relate* when Kate finds a significant other?"

"Harvey's schizoid," Naomi said. She separated her youngest, John Muir Maginnis, from Martha's seal point Siamese. "Don't pull Erica Jong's tail like that, John-John. Physical violence isn't the answer.... I don't know why you're so blown away, though, after the stuff Kate's laid on us in group. Any man that wants his wife to iron his Jockey shorts ... John-John, *stop* that. You're *hurting* Erica. Don't you remember what we told you about *ahimsa,* a loving relationship with the world?"

Martha pushed the coffee plunger, side-stepping John-John, who'd picked up a Sabatier cleaver from her butcher block and was now looking for something to cleave with it. "Well, I kept telling Harvey he was being counterproductive, but he just kept doing this Charlie Manson number. He says he's gonna punch Kate out and shove her contacts down her throat."

Naomi rolled her eyes significantly. "I've always said Harvey had an ongoing problem with fully mature male/female relationships." She suddenly jumped to her feet, alarmed. "Listen, did you see where John-John went? I mean, I just flashed on it; he's still got your cleaver."

Martha followed Naomi into the living room, juggling a Swedish teak tray with the coffee on it, just in time to hear Bill shouting that John John had gone after his *Ficus benjamina.* "Jesus," he roared, "the kid's an *animal.* I mean, how could he cut up a defenseless plant like that? Listen, this is a very sick *Ficus;* it was touch and go for a while after the root shock."

Later, with John-John locked in the bathroom, the four of them talked about parenting. Jason said the problem was that society sent out all these crossed signals. "You try to raise them to be free, and then they get all this *structure* coming down.

Even at Montessori school they make them learn numbers. So what have you got? More *linear thinkers.*"

Martha agreed that the external culture conspired to destroy the natural child. However, she said, there were still alternatives, even if most summer camps for kids were paramilitaries like the Boy Scouts. "You oughta send John-John to Camp Middle Earth," she said. "It's five hundred a week, but it's a *nurturing environment. . . .*"

43. Fear and loathing at Camp Middle Earth

While Gregor enjoyed killing chickens and Tamalpa had a crush on her counselor, Rhododendron, Che hated everything about summer camp. First they routed him out of his tipi at dawn to do yoga out under the redwood trees, and then he was expected to spend the morning chopping firewood for the hot tub. Che missed Martha, TV and Fritos. He wasn't consoled by Sufi dancing and hated the evening soft-encounter groups, when somebody always called him a baby and pointed out that he picked his nose.

Nor did he enjoy survival training, which meant living on things you found in the woods. Huckleberries weren't too bad, though it took him an hour to pick a handful, but acorns were strictly for the birds. Martha didn't give him Fritos at home, but Che knew his way around the Safeway and usually spent his allowance there. At Camp Middle Earth there were no Safeways and money wasn't the medium of exchange. You were supposed to trade your skills for stuff, and Che didn't have any except picking his nose.

Furthermore, the camp was a shuck. Middle Earth didn't have any rules, but Che kept breaking them accidentally, just as he had in group this morning when he refused to tell his peers what he'd dreamed about. Expected to record his dreams in a journal, he used up all the pages instead writing letters home begging for Fritos.

Why hadn't he used his smarts and kept a low profile? Two-thirds of the resource persons, male and female, were doing M.A.'s in behavioral psychology. The slightest sign of what they called "maladjusted socialization," and they insisted on friendly, one-to-one raps about his mother's previous four marriages.

Che kept explaining that four ex-husbands weren't unusual where he lived. He even added cleverly that he believed in "growth and change." Nevertheless, they kept coming on at him about "these hangups caused by identity problems." In desperation, Che asked Gregor to "just make up some stuff" for his dreambook, but Gregor was too busy killing chickens. So Che made the mistake of saying he didn't dream.

Camp Middle Earth felt about not dreaming the way Martha felt about not brushing your teeth. Apparently, if you didn't brush

your teeth, they rotted and fell right out of
your head. Apparently, too, if you didn't
dream, you ended up hopelessly insane.
Che couldn't get to sleep in his tipi because
he was so freaked about meeting his dream
quotient.

Now he was scheduled for Hot Seat Work
in the encounter group that evening, and
when he broke out into a rash, envisioning
himself brought to a rolling boil in the hot
tub, his Surrogate Parent for the session
made him drink a lot of lemon-grass tea.
"Listen, Che," said Mountain Man, "you've
just made a conscious decision. *You're* the
one that decides to get sick or stay healthy.
Listen, you want your body to call the
shots?"

Che just wanted the camp to call Martha
and tell her he'd forgotten his cortisone
ointment. Maybe she'd come and bring it to
him and he could hide out in the trunk of
the Rover. Otherwise he was in for two
more weeks of unstructured freedom that
stopped short of "pharmaceuticals" and doing your own thing if your thing was picking your nose.

Glumly, he consulted the bulletin board,
listing the afternoon's activities, posted outside the communal yurt: belly dancing,
spear fishing and herbal medicine. Che
didn't know what herbal medicine was but
suspected lemon-grass tea was part of it. His
only other choice was pulling organic

weeds in the camp's organic garden, a pastime that only helped promote another eggplant lasagne dinner. If he wanted meat, he had to help kill it; Middle Earth was "into process."

Che crawled back into his tipi and thought about Big Macs in styrofoam boxes, listening furtively to the nearest rock station on his transistor radio, but Mountain Man soon appeared, down on all fours, at the tipi entrance. "Hey, big fella," he said to Che, "why aren't you out there interrelating? This is a *community*, you dig?"

Guiltily, Che snapped off his radio and stuffed it down into his blanket roll. Middle Earth had no electricity and didn't believe in the media hype.

"I'm just meditating," he said. "Just sort of getting in touch with myself."

"*Far out.*" Mountain Man grinned at him. "You're missing a Spontaneous Rap Session, though. We're putting together the last night's graduation boogie. Your little sister's gonna belly dance, and Gregor said he'd help slaughter a sheep."

Che wished Mountain Man would go away so he could take a nap before they put him in the Hot Seat. Every night, when he finally got to sleep, they woke him up for Spontaneous Midnight Cookie Baking.

"Take your finger out of your nose, man. Nose-picking's, like, *uncool*, okay?" Mountain Man began crawling toward him, advancing steadily into the tipi. "Whaddaya say we go have a learning experience? Maybe we could build a tree house, you know?"

Che decided to seize the ball and run with it. Among other things, he was terrified of heights. "Mountain Man, I wanna go *home*," he screamed.

He kept on kicking and screaming like a maniac, with judicious intervals of holding his breath, until Mountain Man finally backed out of the tent. Mountain Man returned with the camp director, Salmon, who'd had to leave the sensory exploration class he was teaching and who chewed Che out for acting like a ten-year-old.

"Yeah, well," Mountain Man said in his

defense, "he's only ten years old, you know?"

Eventually, they let him call Martha, but only after he'd held his breath until he turned blue. Che screamed until Martha promised to come and get him and then he threw in his demand for a Frito fix.

"I can't figure out where his head's at," she told Bill, badly shaken after Che's call. "He kept yelling about how eggplant is yucky, and they were going to throw him down out of a tree. And he's paranoid like you wouldn't believe; he claims they kept him up all night and made him bake carob cookies."

"I'll go get him and you call Steinmetz." Bill already had his car keys in his hand. "God, he really sounds *sick*, you know? I hope we haven't waited too long to get him in therapy. Imagine a ten-year-old kid that can't handle *freedom*. . . ."

44. Ms. Murphy makes her move

When Harvey got the word from Martha that Saturday morning, he called Kate immediately and asked for a divorce. "Twenty years we've been married," he told her, "and a month after you split, you get it on with a *handyperson*. I also hear he's very big on primal therapy. Well, listen, kid, whatever's right. Scream your lungs out if that's what does it for you."

Kate juggled the phone precariously in a hand still slippery with the baby oil she'd been using on Brian's shoulder blades. "Harvey," she said, "have you gone *totally* off your gourd? Wow, I've been waiting for this, you know? I knew sooner or later you'd flip out entirely."

"Yeah, I know. I'm paranoid. You're always telling me how I'm *paranoid*." Harvey decided to throw a rabbit punch; this was no time for *How to Fight Fair*. "Well, from where I'm coming from, *you're* the one that's wiggy. First that ethnic joke with the fake leather suit, and now a 'free-lance handyperson.' Boy, you're heavily into *class*, you know?"

Kate sighed, martyred, on her end of the phone. "That was a *genuine leather* suit, Harvey, and Brian happens to be a beautiful person, but I haven't gone and set up another male dependency. That's just. *typical* of the way your tiny mind works. Listen, after living with you, it's gonna be years before I get clear. Right now I'm practically a walking *trauma.*"

"*Tell* me about it," Harvey shouted. "You think this is a piece of cake on my end? You want trauma, I got trauma. The Maytag overflowed this morning, and you ought to see the family room. It looks like Lake Michigan or something; it's a goddamn urban disaster area."

"Listen, Harvey, who *needs* this? I've got my own problems to work through, you know? So you know what you can do with your Maytag, and don't keep calling me up and hassling me. You made your waterbed and you can lie on it."

Kate slammed down the receiver, leaving Harvey standing there in the kitchen infuriated and waterlogged. Rolling up his pants legs, he went back to the family room, but Lake Michigan was still at high tide and he found himself unable to come to terms with it. He gave up on the bailing and poured some Cutty into a glass instead, thinking about the new morality that had so far cost him his inner serenity, his lower back, his wife and his cat. Harvey thought of Kat Vonnegut, Jr., as a civilian casualty in the sexual revolution.

It boggled him that just a few years ago, he used to come home from the bank in the evenings to find Kate reading the *Ladies' Home Journal* and crying her eyes out over "Can This Marriage Be Saved?" What had happened in the intervening time frame, except for Marlene, Carol and Ms. Murphy?

None of which, of course, was his fault, for now that women were the aggressors, men were simply sexual victims. Maybe he should have carried a hatpin or at least packed Mace in his shoulder bag.

Harvey answered his chiming doorbell expecting the lonely Maytag repairman. He wasn't expecting Stella Murphy, listing slightly under the weight of the ancient Samsonite suitcase she carried. "Hey, hey," she said, taking in his pants legs. "Your costume's really terrific, Harv. What are you doing? Painting your toenails?"

"Stella, what's with the suitcase?" Harvey asked. He freaked before he heard the answer.

Ms. Murphy leaned over and licked him on the ear. "Harv," she said, "I just flashed on it. How I could move in here with you. Like, why should I stay in Sausalito when you've got a great big empty pad?" She dragged the Samsonite over the threshold. "God, talk about tract house city . . . Maybe

we can paint the walls black or something."

Harvey's stockbroker next-door neighbor had stopped trotting back and forth behind his power mower and now stood openly taking in the scene. "Fuller brushperson," Harvey called to him. He pulled Ms. Murphy inside and slammed the door.

Giggling, she licked him on the ear again. "Have I got a free gift for *you*."

Harvey had broken out into a sweat. His Qiana shirt glued itself to his chest. "Stella," he said, "you can't move in here. I mean, I'm just not *ready* for this. Look, I'm still getting over the split-up. I'm practically a walking trauma."

Ms. Murphy was touring the living room. "Tacky," she said. "Wall-to-wall carpet—that's *incredibly* tacky. I'll bet you've even got a Formica breakfast bar. Danish modern in the dining room."

"What's so tacky about Danish modern? It just so happens that table cost a bundle."

"Danish modern's junk, not funk." Ms. Murphy took off her fringed leather jacket, sat down in the Eames chair and kicked off her Frye boots. "Let's just mellow out," she said. "We don't have to start on the walls right away. Hey, roll down your pants legs, will you, Harv? You look like you're wearing pedal pushers."

"Stella, you can't move in here," Harvey said. "Listen, we've got a homeowners' association. It's in the constitution—we can't have orgies. We can't even put our cars up on blocks in the driveway. This is where the action *isn't*, Stella; the action's all in Sausalito."

"Not anymore," Ms. Murphy said. "Wow, I can't *believe* this place. You know what I'll bet you've got in the bedroom? One of those tacky wooden valets. I'll bet you've got a *Water Pik*."

Harvey seized Ms. Murphy's suitcase, intent on putting it back in her VW. "Jesus, what have you got in here, bricks?"

"Just the basics," Stella said. "The new Stevie Wonder. The movie camera. I also brought some incredible weed in case you didn't have enough to go around. I told a few people to make the scene tonight."

"Stella," Harvey said, "I can't get behind this. I keep trying to tell you, I'm really a straight arrow."

"No way. You're really a pussycat. Listen, you're gonna groove on having me here. Shall we get the rest of my stuff out of the car?"

"I'm telling you upfront, you can't move in with me. Take your Samsonite and split." Harvey reached down to pull Stella out of the Eames chair, but she pulled him down into it instead.

"*Incredible*," she said after a while, nuzzling Harvey's sticky neck. "Is that a print of those tacky Van Gogh sunflowers?"

45. Harvey's last stand

Stella Murphy had moved in on Harvey mainly because he was up for grabs, and in the Bay Area, single men who were also straight weren't easy to come by. Witness the want ads in the Marin weekly paper, which no longer solicited secondhand Hide A Beds and baby strollers: "Sensitive Aries, thirty-nine, heavily into personal growth, wants to meet compatible male. Only the able-bodied need apply."

Availability, though, she was finding, was just about all that Harvey had going for him. "God, he's so *neurotic*," she told her stewardess ex-roommate on the phone. "I mean, you ought to see him getting ready for bed. He's got these ratty old pajamas with the seat hanging down around his knees, and this sleep shade so it's dark enough, and his ear plugs and his Sominex. And he sleeps in his ski socks so his feet won't get cold. He looks like a cross between the Lone Ranger and Bigfoot."

"Maybe he doesn't wanna come on like a sex object."

"Not to *worry*," Ms. Murphy said. "Like, I had this housewarming party, you know?

And just when everybody started getting down, where do you think old Harvey went? He locked himself in the bathroom with a bunch of old *Sunsets* and sat there reading 'May in Your Garden.' Here we've got this wild scene going and Harv holes up and reads about earwigs."

"You think he's still got a thing about his ex?"

"I dunno," Ms. Murphy said, "but he's sure got a thing about the cat he creamed. You know, the one that bought the farm when Harvey hit him on his bike? He buried him in this Hush Puppies shoe box out in the backyard, and he just goes out there and stares at the ground. I keep trying to tell him, he's gotta do some Grief Work."

"Stella," said her friend, "you oughta cut him loose. I kept telling you all along, Harvey's a squirrel. Wow, you ever know anybody else who brought his calculator to an orgy?"

"*That's* for sure," Ms. Murphy said. "I just don't know how to give him the word. I guess I'll have to play it by ear and wait until he falls off his bike or something. I mean, maybe his old lady would take him back if something really terrible happened. You think I oughta string a wire across the driveway?"

"Don't do it, Stella. You don't want to *hurt* the dude."

"Yeah, I guess you're right," said Ms.

Murphy, "but I don't wanna spend the best years of my life hanging out with Bigfoot, either. Listen, I better get off the phone. I sent Harv out to buy some more paint, and I just saw his Volvo tooling around the corner."

"Stella," Harvey said unhappily, when he came back into the living room with two more gallons of Midnight Black, "you sure you know what you're doing with the black walls? The goddamn place looks like a bat cave. I keep thinking I oughta hang upside down from the ceiling, you know? How come you couldn't swing with the beige?"

"Beige is *blah,* Harv, it's a nothing color. And anyway, *anything's* an improvement, right? I mean, I don't know where you get off with the beige. Beige walls, beige rug, beige upholstery. The place looked like a dentist's waiting room."

Harvey looked at his transformed tract house. Stella had tacked Indian bedspreads to the ceiling and moved most of the furniture out into the family room, substituting the furry floor pillows she'd brought from her Sausalito apartment. If the place was middle-class tacky before, it now looked like an Algerian restaurant where they made you eat with your hands.

His only consolation, as he got back on his ladder, was that Kat Vonnegut hadn't lived to see it. Although he still hadn't psyched himself up to tell Kate, he now

figured Kat had offed himself on purpose, blaming himself for Kate's defection and committing suicide while on a guilt trip.

The phone rang while he was starting on the hall, and Harvey got down off his ladder to answer it. Stella was forbidden to pick up the phone because Harvey's mother sometimes called from Spokane to ask him if he was "staying regular." Hung up on the importance of such things, she'd once sent him a copy of *Prevention* magazine with the page turned down at an article called "Tales Your Bowels Can Tell You."

Kate's voice came across loud and clear from the pay phone at the Red Cart Market, two blocks and two minutes away from the house. "I was doing my grocery shopping," she said, "because the Red Cart has these terrific veggies, and I flashed that I needed my asparagus steamer. The Revere Ware was a wedding present on *my* side. So I thought I'd just swing by and get it, because you could never relate to asparagus anyhow."

"Kate," Harvey said wildly, "stay where you are. I'll bring you the goddamn asparagus steamer, only don't come by the house, okay? It's full of bugs. I'm coming down with swine flu."

"Harvey," Kate said, "you're a *total* hypochondriac. I don't think you're coming down with swine flu; it's probably just male chauvinist piggism."

"Very funny. Listen, I've got a fever. You wanna start an epidemic?"

"I don't wanna start *anything*, Harvey, so don't *you* start anything, okay? That's my asparagus steamer and I'm coming to get it. And you can also get out the cat carrier while you're at it, because I want custody of Kat."

Harvey faced the inevitable. "Yeah," he said, "I can dig it."

With two minutes to go till blast-off, he raced around the house in a frenzy, locking all the outside doors and bundling Ms. Murphy, protesting, into the den. "You come out of there," he said vehemently, "and you're gonna end up in a Hush Puppies box. I did it before and I can do it again."

"Harv," Ms. Murphy said, "what are you freaking out about? You're a consenting adult, remember?"

Harvey threatened her with extinction, grabbed the asparagus steamer and took up a defensive position just inside the front door. Kate rang the doorbell while he was still frantically preparing his opening remarks.

"When the going gets tough, the tough get going," Harvey remembered somebody saying. He pulled himself together and reached for the doorknob. Then he remembered that Nixon had said it, and that when the going had got tough, he'd gone into exile at San Clemente. . . .

46. Darkness at noon

As soon as Harvey opened the door, Kate knew something weird was coming down. First of all he'd locked her out; she heard him turning the latch and undoing the dead bolt. Then he opened the door no more than an inch and peered out at her with one beady eye. "Harvey," she said, "this is ridiculous; you don't have to be so paranoid. I'm not packing a Saturday-night special, *really*. I just want my asparagus steamer."

Harvey said in a croak that he wasn't being paranoid, he just didn't want to breathe on her. "You don't wanna get what I've got," he said. "I think it's Legionnaires' disease. Listen, the minute you split, I'm going back to bed. I think I oughta get off my feet."

Kate said he could also get off her back. "I'm through doing that chicken soup number, so don't try to play on my sympathy, Harvey. My guess is you're just hungover; you tied one on again last night. Well, take two aspirin. Take your lumps. Alice doesn't *live* here anymore."

"Hey," Harvey said, "that's really uncalled for; there isn't any *call* for that. I'm just thinking about your health, you know? You don't have to be so goddamn hostile; I've got the asparagus steamer right here."

He whipped the door open and pushed the steamer into Kate's arms, retreating immediately behind an opening no wider than the white of his eye. Who did he think he was, the Sutton Manor flasher?

"Harvey, what's going on?" Kate demanded.

"Well, *actually*, I'm doing some painting," Harvey said, "and the joint is kind of torn apart. It's occupational therapy. I've been sort of bummed out all alone, so I thought I'd paint the living room."

Kate tried to push the door open wider. "This I've gotta see," she said, squinting into the gloom. "Harvey, for God's sake, what have you *done*? What color are you painting my walls?"

"Black," Harvey said defensively. "I'm painting them black, because I happen to think the beige was blah. Anyway, it's no skin off your back. Alice doesn't *live* here anymore."

Kate rushed the door and shoved it open. The hall was so impenetrable she couldn't tell Harvey from the coat rack. "This is *unbelievable*," she said. "What the hell are you doing, starting a worm farm?"

"Listen, you've got your asparagus steamer, so go steam some asparagus, okay?

I can do my own interior decorating."

Kate was taking in Ms. Murphy's furry floor pillows and the Indian bedspreads on the ceiling. "Yeah, you've got a beautiful talent," she said. "It looks like an Algerian cathouse. Which reminds me, have you got Kat squared away? I mean it, Harvey, I'm taking him home with me."

Harvey improvised. "I couldn't find him. I think he's out catting around or something. Listen, how about a beer at Sid & Jim's? We've got a lot to talk about. Like, your mother called the other night, and I didn't want to give her the word, so I told her you were in the hospital. She wanted to get on a plane and come down here, but I said it was just hemorrhoids."

"Harvey, that's absolutely *disgusting*."

"Yeah, well, I just flashed on hemorrhoids off the wall. Next time I'll make it a brain tumor. Look, you want that beer or not?"

Kate was starting down the hall, looking for the furniture. Harvey traced her movements by the gleam of the asparagus steamer. "Don't go back there," he said desperately. "We've got army ants; I'm fumigating like crazy."

"You've got somebody here, haven't you, Harvey?" Kate came to a halt and turned to confront him. "Some little checkout chick from Safeway, or maybe that teller from the bank, the one that wears the ankle bracelets. How many does it take to go around one of her ankles? I mean, I couldn't help noticing when I picked you up for lunch one day, and she was practically crawling all over you. She's got legs like King Kong."

Harvey grabbed Kate by the sleeve of her caftan and pulled her back into the living room. Behind the den door was Stella Murphy in her too tight "Born to Boogie" T-shirt. "Kate," he said, playing his last card, "here's the good news: I'm all alone. The bad news is I killed Kat Vonnegut. I hit him on my bike and he cashed in his chips."

Kate burst into tears. "Harvey, how *could* you?"

"Listen, I feel *terrible*. I really miss that dude, you know? I mean, since you left we'd really gotten close. Sort of like *The Odd Couple*. I took him with me to McDonald's every night, and I had a Big Mac and he had a fishburger. Hold the bun and light on the tartar sauce."

Kate enveloped him in her caftan. "You poor *baby*, Harvey," she said. "You must have been on an *incredible* guilt trip."

"I was at first," Harvey admitted. "Then I thought, it wasn't *my* fault. I tried to teach him not to chase bikes."

Kate was rummaging in the pocket in which he kept his handkerchief. Harvey stroked her hair while she blew her nose. "Hey, Kate, whaddaya say?" he said. "You think we could get our act together again?

The other night I was doing the taxes, and it almost killed me, filing a joint return like that and you getting it on with a handyperson and Kat buried out in the yard in this shoe box. . . . I keep meaning to plant some perennials on top of him. . . . And Joannie gone, and Donald Barthelme, and Christmas season coming up. You know I always freak out at Christmas. Seasonal holiday depression."

Kate was weeping noisily. She still clutched her Revere Ware asparagus steamer, which dug uncomfortably into Harvey's soft underbelly. "I'm not getting it on with Brian," she said. "Brian uses my *hair dryer*, Harvey. And the furnace where I live broke down, so you know what I think about when I'm lying there too cold to sleep at night? I think about our double bed and the electric blanket with the dual controls."

Over Kate's shoulder, Harvey, horrified, saw the door to the den swinging slowly open. He freed one arm and semaphored frantically, but Stella Murphy sauntered out into the hall anyway.

"Does anybody mind if I split?" she said. "And get yourself another secretary, Harv. I'm not gonna work for a worm farm. . . ."

47. Kate's inner resources

Martha, Naomi and Marlene were having lunch at Henderson's Grandmother and comparing notes on Kate and Harvey. "I've gotta hand it to Kate," Naomi said. "I'll admit it right upfront, I didn't know she had all those inner resources."

Martha nodded. "Just off the wall she comes on like a lightweight. I used to think she had a pretty dim bulb myself, but she's just fantastic in a crisis situation, and she's had some heavy-duty help. She's seeing a Life Goals Consultant at the Wellness Resource Center, and of course she's also working with Harvey's shrink. Right now he thinks Harvey's mother laid this trip on him about how sex was dirty, and Harvey's been trying to rewrite the script."

"He told me some *incredible* stuff about his mother." Marlene poured more Tiger's Milk out of her Thermos. "Wow, it really blew me away. Do you know every time he got a cold, she rubbed his chest with Mentholatum? That tells you something about where he's coming from."

"Yeah, well, *imagine* how Kate felt when

Harvey had her conned like that and then this fox came out of the den." Martha signaled the waitress for more wine. "She said she flashed on it right away, though, that he was having a nervous breakdown. He wasn't tracking. He was all over the board."

"So how could she tell?" Naomi said. "Harvey's *always* all over the board."

"Hey, you're *great*," Martha told the waitress. She poured herself another glass of the house red. "Well, I guess he just started gibbering about this international conspiracy of women, and how they'd planted Ms. Murphy in his office and Elizabeth Ray in the Senate office building, and they had a hit squad that offed his cat. God, I knew he was paranoid, but I didn't know he was *that* far gone."

"Wow, poor Kate. How did she *deal* with it?" Marlene was thinking that six months ago, she could have been in Kate's Birkenstocks; privately, she blamed Harvey's freak-out on a lecithin deficiency.

"I think she called an ambulance. She was still pretty hyper by the time she got to our house, so I didn't hit her with too many questions, and anyway, we had a wild scene going ourselves. We'd just brought Gregor home from Middle Earth, and somehow he'd gotten hold of this Coleman lantern. . . ."

"Hey," Naomi said, "you're *all* over the board, Martha. How did Kate get rid of Elizabeth Ray?"

"It wasn't *that* bad," Martha said. "She told Kate she types thirty words a minute. Anyway, Kate had to help her move, because she has this little VW bug and she couldn't get all her floor pillows in it. They ended up at the bar at The Seven Seas, and I guess the two of them finally got clear. Kate says it wasn't really her fault; she's just been programmed, like the rest of us. *Her* mother told her sex was terrific."

Marlene stared pensively into her Tiger's Milk. "People shouldn't be allowed to *have* kids, you know?"

Naomi was busy with her pocket calculator. "Let's see, I had the spinach-and-leek soup, and Martha had the carrot cake. . . ."

"I'm treating," Martha said expansively. "Bill just pulled down a mini-park at some big oil refinery over in Richmond. He says they're trying to upgrade the corporate image, and they just gave him a bundle and told him to do his thing."

Kate was out in the backyard meditating when Martha's Rover pulled into the driveway, Naomi having suggested that the three of them drop by and offer her some peer-group support. She made a pot of herbal tea and served it on her Brown Jordan patio table. "Well," she said, "there's light at the end of the tunnel. Harvey's making terrific progress; I just came back from visiting hours. He's only had one major setback and that was when Jerry from the car pool stopped by to see him in this 'Born to Boogie' T-shirt. He's getting a hold on reality again, though. He's talking about going back into escrow."

Naomi stared at Kate intensely. "How do *you* feel about that, *really?*"

"I don't think he oughta rush it," Kate said. "He's got all this sick leave coming at Wells Fargo, and they don't expect him back for a while. I said he was having these hemorrhoids removed."

"Kate," Martha asked, "are you going to

take him back? I mean, once they get him tracking again?"

Kate avoided eye-to-eye contact. Her gaze wandered off into the pyracantha. "I'm working through that right now," she said. "I keep thinking, maybe the system works. I mean, you've got a viable marriage, Martha."

"What I've got is a viable husband, and this is *número* five, you know? The other four times I couldn't make it fly. I just happened to luck out totally, finally, and meet a dude with his head on straight. Hey, what happened to Brian from the house? The one with those incredible pectorals?"

Kate got busy with the teapot. "I told him it wouldn't fly," she said. "I'm a Sagittarius and he's a Leo."

"Oh, *wow*." Marlene looked thoroughly alarmed. "I've never met a Leo that wasn't bad news."

"I've also got a *terrific* lot of psychic energy invested in the marriage. I talked it over with my counselor, and he says *he* thinks Harvey and I could probably get it together, but only, *only* with a whole new scenario. He says I've gotta define my expectations, so I've been working on it. I'm making a list."

"Stick to one-syllable words," said Naomi. "Look, I'm sorry to break this up, but I'm taking a class in Mongolian hot-pot cookery and I promised to bring the

[288]

cellophane noodles." She took Kate aside when they got out to the car. "I'm going to ask you an *intimate* question, Kate. Do you have absolute *total* confidence in the Wellness Resource Center? Because I know a *beautiful* human being at the Center for Designed Change. When Jason had his fortieth birthday, I called him, and he came right up to the house instanter the minute I mentioned the suicide threat."

"Thanks but no thanks," Kate said bravely. "I mean, I've finally come to terms with it; *I'm* the one that's gotta make it happen." She waved them around the corner and then went back to her list of non-negotiable demands. "*Número uno*," she wrote in her Italic script. "Cut out the Cutty *totally....*"

48. An offer
Harvey can't refuse

"Harvey," Kate said, the day she brought him home from the psychiatric ward, "you mustn't feel guilty. *Really.* I mean, mental illness isn't a stigma anymore. The way I look at it, a nervous breakdown is just nature's way of telling you you've freaked."

Harvey said he didn't want to talk about it. "My shrink says I'm still terribly *vulnerable,* and I shouldn't do too much soul-searching, you know? I thought I'd just sort of have a Cutty. I'm supposed to get back to my normal routine right away."

"No Cutty, Harvey," Kate said firmly. "That Cutty number's got to go. Anyway, you can't mix booze and Librium. Don't you remember *Valley of the Dolls?*"

"Yeah, well, I guess I'll go watch the tube. They let me watch the tube at the hospital."

"*Terrific,*" Kate said. "You just get home and all you wanna do is vegetate in front of the TV. No way. You're supposed to keep busy; occupational therapy."

Harvey told her he'd found pro football on television "terrifically therapeutic. It's a great way to release your aggression. You watch those linebackers zap the quarterback and you don't have to go around acting out. Kicking little kids or something. They *made* us watch the 49ers. Absolutely mandatory."

"You can act out painting the living room, Harvey, so get up that ladder and boogie. And don't try to give me any flak; I'm through living in a septic tank."

Harvey said he wasn't really into walls. "I think I'd like to segue into landscapes." He registered Kate's implacable expression and tried a diversionary tactic. "Hey, I'm ready to get behind some down home cooking. How about making me a salami sandwich?"

Kate sat down on a stool at the breakfast bar and crossed her legs in their Danskin leotards; despite all the Cutty under the dam, Harvey noticed wistfully, his wife still had terrific wheels.

"I'd like to get *clear* on a few things," Kate said. "I think it's time for some in-depth discussion. I'm not going back to the same old lifestyle with you cracking wise and putting me down and me making salami sandwiches all the time."

"I'll go for tuna fish," Harvey said amiably.

"So if you want me to hang in there any longer, you're gonna have to bring your energies to reconstituting this marriage *totally*."

Harvey muttered that he didn't know the marriage was still freeze-dried. "I'm not

ready for this," he said. "I'm still on the thin edge of the wedge, you know? Furthermore, we can't afford to put me away again; it's not covered by the group insurance. My shrink put down on the medical form that my paranoia was a preexisting condition."

"Exactamente," Kate said coldly, "which is why you're gonna have to get it together. Don't think just because I'm coming back to you, I'm going to let you mess my mind over again. You're the heavy in all this, Harvey, and *you're* the one that's got to shape up."

"For sure, for sure; I'm outa shape. I think I'll get on the old Motobecane and pedal up a storm out to Point Reyes station. You wanna come along in the bus in case I need a sag wagon?"

Kate was attaching a memorandum to the refrigerator door with smiley-face magnets. "This is my list of conditions," she said. "Absolutely mandatory. One of them is that you cut out the bike tripping on weekends. I've had it with the bicycle widow bit; from now on, I want us to do things *together*. Marriage is supposed to be a working partnership."

Harvey thought of telling her that you could rent tandem bicycles out at Inverness. Then he flashed that in their working partnership, Kate held at least 51 percent of the stock. "I can relate," he said, resigned. "Take the goddamn list from the top." No way did he want Kate to split again, leaving him to the tract house and his own devices; not with Ms. Murphy still on the prowl somewhere in the urban jungle.

"Item one you already know about. *Pas de* booze, Harvey, and I really mean it. You've been using Cutty as a *crutch*."

"Got it," Harvey said morosely. "I take my Librium and throw away my crutches."

"Item two, no more screwing around. This time I want a total commitment."

"What you see is what you get. I mean, you want a total commitment, you've got it."

"Item three, I'm taking back my maiden name. I'm tired of being a *nonperson*, Harvey."

"I wouldn't stand in your way," Harvey said, "but I think you're making a terrible mistake. 'Kate Smith' . . . Wow, you're gonna get all those calls again from people who want you to sing 'God Bless America' at VFW conventions."

"Item four is the bicycle number, and that brings us to item five," Kate said. "Item five is the big one, okay? I want us to renew our marriage vows. *Publicly*. Surrounded by our friends. Naomi says what's wrong with our lives—I mean *everybody's* lives in the twentieth century—is we've done away with ritual, you know? and we haven't come up with anything to replace it. Ritualwise, we're living in a vacuum."

"I dunno," Harvey said thoughtfully.

"We've still got 'Honk if you love Jesus.' Anyway, didn't we get married *once?* I thought it was like the Bay Area Funeral Society: you pay the money and you're signed up for life."

"I'm gonna want your input about the ceremony, so let me have your thinking," Kate said. She got down off the kitchen stool; her leotards made a slithering noise that Harvey found a total turn-on. "Harvey," she said, putting her arms around him, "I just keep thinking that this time, *hopefully,* we can make marriage *work,* you know?"

Harvey had popped a Librium while Kate read her list of non-negotiable demands. Hugging her back, he thought serenely that Naomi was probably right about ritual. Next time he saw her, he intended to rely on ancient tradition and give her the finger. . . .

49. Martha's Marin Christmas

Martha blamed the collapse of her fifth marriage partly on Kate and Harvey Holroyd and partly on the Christmas season in Marin, a one-long-party marathon out of *They Shoot Horses, Don't They?*

She went directly to Naomi's house after Bill had packed his bag, taken his *Ficus benjamina* and moved back into the Edgewater Inn, and over Ernie's house-label Chablis, unburdened herself to Naomi at length.

"What *happened* was, we went to the Gallaghers', and that was the second party for the day, and we had to make the scene at two more, and Bill was pushed out of shape about it. He said that the goddamn holidays reminded him of the roller derby and he wouldn't go to Tony Wilson's because last year he O.D.'d on eggnog. You know that eggnog Tony makes with whipping cream and fertilized eggs? Bill says it gave him the trots for weeks and his cholesterol level shot up to flashpoint. So I told him we *had* to go to Tony's because the Wilsons just split up and if we just went to Marsha's party, they'd figure we were taking sides.

"So *he* said why did Tony and Marsha have to have open houses the same day, and *I* said that was the problem all along: lack of real communication. I also told him he didn't have to worry about Marsha Wilson serving eggnog. She *hates* the stuff; it gives her canker sores. She just never had the nerve to tell Tony.

"*Anyway*, we got to the Gallaghers' and right away it was all downhill. They were playing that Joan Baez Christmas record that Bill says drives him straight up the wall, and they had the stereo doing 'Carol of the Drums' over and over on automatic replay. And for some reason they *happened* to be serving eggnog, which I can't figure, because before, they've always done the hot buttered rum number. And the quiche was all gone; we'd gotten there late."

"Martha," Naomi said, "watch your wine. John-John's a wine freak; he just made a pass at it."

Through her tears, Martha continued. "So we hadn't had anything to eat at Angela Stein's because Angela makes this beef tartare with a raw egg in the middle of it and Bill just freaks when he's in the same room. I guess that's why the eggnog got to him. God, you should have *heard* the way he came on. The Gallaghers just got back from Iran, and Frank was trying to tell him about it, and Bill just kept making these snide remarks, like had Frank ever seen

Novato at sunset. Honestly, I could have *died*."

Naomi grabbed John-John by the ear, took Martha's glass out of his hand and filled it with Chablis again. "Try to *focus*, Martha," she said. "I still don't know what really came down."

"Well, Kate and Harvey came in, you know? Kate looked *terrific*, by the way. She was wearing the 'survival look,' with her pants tucked into her hiking boots and this magnetic compass instead of a watch. Boy, she knows I. Magnin's the way I know the back of my hand, you know? So Bill went over to talk to Harvey, and Harvey was drinking carrot juice. He told Bill they kept him zonked on Librium and he couldn't drink booze or he had these flashbacks. He also kept staring up at the ceiling all the time, because Kate made him paint the living room again and his back developed vapor lock or something."

"Martha, listen, your nose is running. I knew you'd want to know about it." Naomi followed Martha into the bathroom, where Martha blew her nose and kept on talking.

"Bill's incredibly *sensitive*," she said. "I guess he must have identified with Harvey, because he told me afterward how he told Harvey he couldn't let women roll all over him. So Harvey tells him he already knows that; it's 'non-negotiable demand number two.'"

"You're losing me," Naomi said. "I'm trying to relate, but you're losing me."

"Oh, wow, I'm sorry. I'm just so *upset*. God, I could *strangle* Harvey, you know?" Martha plunged blindly through the house back to the kitchen, scattering bits of sodden Kleenex. "Hey, what happened to my wineglass? Well, *anyway*, Kate made Harvey a list of stuff he had to get behind, and they're also gonna renew their marriage vows. At Falkirk, with caterers. Live music, the whole shot. Kate says she knows this guy Harold from the house who can get her Too Loose Lautrec, you know? *I* said *I* thought it sounded super and that was when we got into a hassle. By that time we were on our way to Tony's and Bill threw this *incredible* scene; he said Harvey was practically a clone and the whole thing was just like *Catch-22*.

"*I* said how could he get behind Harvey after the way he'd treated Kate, and *he* said he *happened* to be behind the steering wheel and I could either cool it or get out and walk. Meanwhile he's all over the goddamn *freeway*. He tried to pass this Peterbilt and I thought, wow, we've bought it for sure."

"God, it's *awful*," Naomi said. "Men are so irresponsible in automobiles; they just can't handle all that power."

"So we get to Tony's and right away, Bill starts telling everybody that Kate had Harvey lobotomized. And Tony started in about Marsha and how she'd left him a hollow shell. Did you know that when Marsha split she took *both* Lufthansa and Sabena? I mean, I've gotta go along with it—that was really a bit *much*."

"*Lufthansa* and *Sabena?*" Naomi said.

"The basset hounds. She took both the bassets. Well, about the time Bill called Kate 'Big Nurse,' I decided I'd *had* it, you know? I mean, all this time I'd thought Bill was centered, and suddenly, wow, it absolutely zapped me. I'd married another MCP, and he was gonna be the *role model* for Tamalpa. Right upfront on the way to Marsha's, I told him I wanted a trial separation. Like, he'd already said he didn't love me."

"Bill said *that?*" Naomi said, amazed. "That really blows my mind completely. I thought you had this *total* commitment."

"He didn't actually say he didn't *love* me." Martha drank some Chablis out of the jug. "What he *actually* said was that he thought we had a high incompatibility quotient."

"Martha, take it easy on the wine." Naomi moved the Ernie's out of reach. "I know you're really in the pits, but getting sloshed isn't gonna help. Why don't you call Bill's ex Vivian? Bill must be just *full* of anxieties; maybe Vivian can give you some insight."

"Vivian's in Tibet," Martha said. "They're taking this guided tour with Sherpas." She pulled herself together and lit a cigarette. "I guess it'll level out *somehow*, you know? I mean, we're going to all the same Christmas parties. . . ."

50. Taking the cosmic overview

"God, I feel just *terrible*," Kate said. "I thought Martha and Bill had a good thing going. Martha says it was on the surface, though. They never really got down to the wellsprings."

Harvey looked at her warily over the top of his book. Kate had given him *Predictable Crises of Adult Life* for Christmas, and somehow he expected a pop quiz. "Yeah, well, you never know," he said. "I mean, you never really *know*."

"For sure. Apparently Bill was *terribly* immature. Vivian told Martha he'd never really found himself. She said he'd never even really looked."

Kate had given up smoking again as one of her New Year's resolutions and now munched out on sunflower seeds as substitute oral gratification. The steady crunch-crunch drove Harvey up the wall. He wondered if Kate would go for having her jaws wired shut.

"Martha's swinging with it, though; she says her tarot reader told her how the whole number was in the cards. She's back in therapy, and she's seeing a lot of Brian, and

Brian's being *incredibly* supportive. He says she *basically* has a lot of ego strength; she just needs a lot of reinforcement."

Harvey closed his book in midcrisis. He said he thought that what Martha needed, "*personally,*" was a punch in the mouth.

"Harvey, did you take your two-o'clock?" Kate asked suspiciously. She kept tabs on Harvey's tranquilizers because he came on hostile when he missed one. "Listen, I thought you *liked* the Valium. You said it didn't make you spacy like the Librium."

"I love the Valium," Harvey said. "I'm just getting tired of walking into stuff. Like, I like the nose I've *got*, you know? I hate to keep creaming it that way. This morning I bent over to pull on my socks and I took this header right onto the rug. I thought maybe I ought to kick the Valium. See if I could maintain cold turkey."

Kate had already gone to the kitchen for Harvey's pill and couldn't hear him over the running water. "There isn't any cold turkey," she said, coming back with the Valium and a glass.

Under the guise of running the errands, Harvey floated out to his Volvo and pointed it toward downtown Mill Valley, thinking vaguely of having a Heineken. Once there, however, he couldn't face a fern bar and ended up blinking in the sun on the bench in front of the savings and loan. Mill Valley was changing rapidly as the bars went out

and the plant stores came in, and what bars remained resembled plant stores. You didn't know whether to order a beer or a coleus.

Some things, however, remained immutable, despite the Chamber of Commerce and its recent "Paint Up, Clean Up" campaign. Harvey took in the heady Mill Valley gestalt: the steam rising over the hydra-spa and clouding the glass roof of the Physical Therapy Center, where Kate currently went for deep foot massage; the tennis types with their status tans, enhanced, in January, by windburn and goose bumps; the pushers out in front of the Book Depot. Harvey watched one of them making a sale, cheerfully accepting an Amex credit card, and recognized Joan's old boyfriend Spenser. Upwardly mobile, Spenser now carried his wares in a monogrammed Mark Cross brief-case.

"Oh, hiya, man," Spenser said, when Harvey went over to him. "What's coming down, like, back at the ranch-style?" He scrutinized Harvey closely through his shades. "Hey, what are you *doing* these days? You really look spacey."

"I'm doing Valium," Harvey said. "Listen, Spenser, you heard from Joan?"

"Naw," Spenser said. "Just the one post-card. *Valium*, wow. That stuff's *poison*. Hey, man, things go better with coke."

"Where was the card from?" Harvey asked frantically, over Spenser's lunatic giggles. Mainly to keep him from demateri-alizing, he grabbed a handful of Spenser's Harley-Davidson T-shirt, but Spenser im-mediately freaked.

"Don't *touch* me," he shouted at Harvey. "I can't stand body contact, you know? And don't call me Spenser. I hate to be called *Spenser*." He writhed out of Harvey's grasp and bopped around on the sidewalk. "Hey, you wanna get in on the good stuff? I'm having an after-Christmas sale."

Harvey threatened Spenser with grievous bodily harm.

"Aw, *man*," Spenser said reproachfully, "whaddaya wanna trash me for? You want the postcard, you can have the postcard.

I've got it here in my goodie bag some-place."

Spenser rummaged among the Ziploc bags in his briefcase and produced Joan's card. "Amsterdam a trip," it said.

"Joan's in *Holland?*" Harvey asked, mind-boggled.

"No, man, Amsterdam. She's in Amsterdam. It says right there on the postcard, you dig?" Spenser, like Joan, had gone to Tam High. "Amsterdam's not in Holland, it's in *Europe.*"

Kate was rapping on the phone when Harvey came charging back into the house. "Joan's in *Amsterdam,*" he said to her. "I can't believe it. Can you believe it?"

"I can't *believe* it," Kate said into the phone. "Joan's in Amsterdam, isn't that in-credible? Harvey just made the scene and told me. He must have had a flash or something. Listen, Martha, I'll catch you later." She hung up and stared admiringly at Harvey. "Harvey, that's *unbelievable,*" she said. "You must be just terribly psychic. Like Uri Geller. I'll bet you can bend *spoons.*"

"Actually I'm more into car keys. Look, I saw Spenser down at the Depot, except he doesn't wanna be called Spenser anymore. He said I could call him 'Ronald' or 'Super-freak.' Anyway, he laid ·this postcard on me."

Kate read the message and then looked at

the picture. "God, it looks so *Dutch*," she said. "Listen, we can go through the consulate. Get Joannie home in time for the ceremony. Martha says we ought to have it the first day of spring, because spring's the time for growth and renewal. And here's the beauty part: we can renew *our* marriage vows on Martha's first anniversary."

Harvey was grateful for the Valium. "I thought Martha and Bill were *splitting*."

"Harvey, can't you *see?*" Kate said. "They're splitting. We're getting married again. It's all personal growth. Evolving *Process.* . . ."

51. Growth and renewal: the beauty part

Kate was having lunch with Carol, somewhat self-conscious as the two of them munched out on Yet Wah's potstickers, because of the way people stared at Carol's crew cut. Carol now lived out at Synanon, having "finally found the answer. The Games are what really did it for me," she said. "I mean, what you've got is this whole community of people who *care* enough to tear you apart."

Kate herself tried not to stare at Carol's head. Different strokes, and what really mattered, in the final analysis, was that Carol had got clear. Getting clear was the bottom line.

"Listen, it's *incredible*," Kate said, "the heavy changes we've all gone through. I was making out my guest list, you know, for the Celebration of Open Commitment, and nobody, but *nobody* we know is in the same space anymore. My whole address book is totally inoperative."

"*Really.*" Carol speared a potsticker. "It blows me away to think about it. I can't get over Joan, for instance; wow, that must have been *some* mystical breakthrough. The way she just sort of flashed on how she wants to be a dental hygienist."

"For sure. We thought it was weird at first; we had a lot of trouble relating. She's always had a *thing* about teeth, though, even as a little kid, and she's got this terrific digital dexterity. She says she was hanging out in the Vondel Park and all of a sudden it hit her: zap! She knew what she wanted to do with her life."

"Far out," Carol said. "*Fantastic*. Listen, speaking of going through changes, what's coming down with Angela Stein? I saw her out at Bolinas the other day, *jogging*, for God's sake. Angela Stein *jogging*. Sam used to say she was so nonphysical she wouldn't even read hard-bound books. She waited till they came out in paperback so it wasn't so much work schlepping them around."

"I dunno, but she's running up a storm, and she's very big on the Physical Therapy Center. She even gave me a gift certificate for Christmas." Kate dug around in her purse and found it: "A new path to health has been opened to you. . . . May you continue to grow in balanced harmony. . . . Please call to learn about your new options in life."

"I thought it was a nice gesture, you know? but I haven't gotten behind it yet. I gained all this weight when I gave up the ciggies; my muscle tone is practically zilch. Hey, did I fill you in on the Wilsons? Tony moved to Mendocino. He's got this hot-tub franchise or something, and he's also doing free-lance Traegaring."

"Free-lance *what*? I mean, is that like Shiatsu?"

"Sort of," Kate said. "*Kind of* like. Psychophysiological clearing through integrative structural balancing. I think Shiatsu's more *Oriental*, though. And Marsha's teaching creative aggression. You know, how to assert your self without guilt?"

"What about Martha and Bill?" Carol asked. "Boy, do I feel sorry for Martha. All those marriages. All those divorces. She's just *compulsive* about repeating the same old self-destructive patterning."

Kate resolutely pushed away her plate and then decided she'd just eat the cashews off her chicken. Nuts were a good source of useable protein. "Martha's pretty together," she said. "She's getting it on with Brian from the house and he's got her doing primal screaming. She's also just been born again."

Carol dropped her chopsticks. "Martha's gotten *religion*?"

"*God*, no, not *that* born again. The kind where you reexperience the birth trauma. *Very* heavy; you have to be ready for it. You've got this guide—it's this place in the city with a lot of mats and stuff on the floor—and you curl up in the fetal position. . . ."

"I'm superinterested, but not over lunch."

"Or you can also do it in a tank of warm water. . . . Hey, don't you want your other potsticker?"

"How about Bill? Husband *número cinco?*"

"Living with Vivian, his ex, and Vivian's second husband," Kate said. "Isn't that *totally* terrific? He used to be so hostile, you know? And now he's coming to terms with Vivian as part of his total life experience. I guess he also got tired of the Edgewater. You know how tight apartments are in Marin."

"Yeah, but who could live anywhere else? Marin's this whole high-energy trip with all these happening people," Carol said. "Can you imagine spending your life out there in the wasteland someplace? Like, I went to this garage sale last weekend: live music, hot hors d'oeuvres, Parducci Vineyards Gamay Beaujolais. *Wow*, I said to myself, *only* in Marin. This is where it's at, you know?"

Kate felt a little stab of anxiety. It hadn't occurred to her that in scheduling her Celebration of Open Commitment for prime time on a weekend, she was going to be competing with garage sales, which got more boffo all the time. She herself had recently picked up an Eric Norstad vase at a three-family spectacular catered by Caravansary.

"I hear you," she said. "Look, I've gotta split. Marlene is doing the food for Falkirk and we've got to interface about the menu. Did I tell you she's giving organic cooking classes? Making it big. She says her whole *thrust* is conceptualizing the body as this living organism full of organisms. So what you do is, instead of feeding your face, you think of yourself as an entire ecosystem."

Carol ran manicured fingers through her crew cut. "Kate," she said, "it's really been a groove. Not just the lunch; the overview. Boy, have we all broken *loose* this year. Even Harvey, and right upfront, I thought Harvey was strung out for keeps. I just thought being uptight was his karma."

"Well," said Kate, "the Valium helps. And of course I'm giving him lots of space. Hey, do you mind if I eat the last pot-sticker? I've got this total case of the munchies."

"Over to you; I'm not very hungry." Carol got a little unsteadily to her feet. "I keep flashing on that birth-trauma bit, and the mats, and the tank of warm water, you know? I guess I just wasn't *ready* for it. . . ."

52. Kate and Harvey begin again

Kate Smith and Harvey Holroyd
request your presence
at a Spring Festival—
a Celebration of Open Commitment and
Feeling Exchange where we can just *Be*.
Come reaffirm with us our belief
that in Life, it's the Journey that counts,
not the Goal.

Falkirk
(the old Robert Dollar mansion)
March 21st, three o'clockish p.m.

Kate's friend Rita from Lagunitas summed up the collective feedback about Kate's and Harvey's gala at Falkirk. "Wasn't the whole thing just *outrageous*?"

Kate presided over the gathering, radiant in flowing chiffon. "It's all very loose," she told the guests, as they converged on the old Victorian house. "Just get yourself some champagne and hang out. The whole thing's gonna be *totally* laid back; we'll just write the scenario as the party goes along."

She and Harvey had invited seventy people: Harvey's car pool and Kate's consciousness-raising group; heavies from the Marin rock royalty who knew Joan and Spenser; shrinks, sex therapists, est alumni, Kate's TA and TM instructors; vegetarians, masseurs, Kate's new hairdresser, Mr. Rudolph, friends from previous incarnations before she and Harvey had really begun to explore their options.

"God," said Carol, who made the scene in a thirties dress and a sequined skullcap covering up her Synanon crew cut. "I can't help it, I *love* it. It's so *decadent.*"

Harvey was in charge of the champagne, and though he looked stoned, was in his element. "It's Spanish, actually," he told people. "I think it's got more nose than Mumm's and more *esprit* than Laurent Perrier."

He himself was drinking carrot juice. Valium and champagne were a wipe-out.

"Kate," said Angela Stein ecstatically, "this is really outasight. Wow, Marlene must have cooked her head off. The tabbouleh, all that whole-wheat lasagne, the millet stroganoff, the brown rice and veggies. I just had one of those soybean canapés, and I wanna tell you, they're something *else.*"

Kate was pretty high on the whole scene herself as she gazed out over the crowd she'd assembled. Only in marvelous Marin, and thank God she didn't live in the boonies. She couldn't take all the credit, though; The Secret Garden had done the flowers, Marlene catered the buffet, and when Harold dropped the ball on the music, Martha somehow rounded up a Moog synthesizer and two electric guitars. "Not to worry," she reassured Kate. "The dude on the Moog can really *wail*."

Tony Wilson, in coveralls and beard, made the scene from Mendocino. Tony was "into a whole new lifestyle. Right now I'm building this organic shelter. No doors, no roof, nothing faky. Most of it is a skills exchange; like, this guy built me a lean-to for the Porsche and I'm letting him have a hot tub at a discount."

Martha came escorted by Brian but did a turned-on hustle with Bill while Brian danced with Bill's ex, Vivian. "No percentage in being bitter," Martha told Kate philosophically. "I mean, Bill's still a terrific dancer. Hey, I just saw Joan and Spenser. How come Spenser's carrying a briefcase?"

At seven o'clock with the party getting down, Harvey came and took Kate aside. "We're running out of the bubbly," he said. "Maybe we ought to get married or something."

Kate agreed and went to find the Reverend Thurston on the dance floor, where he was rocking out with Marlene. "Remember," she said, "just off the wall, the way we

dialogued about it. We want something, you know, *dynamic* but unstructured."

"Right on, I hear you," Thurston said. When Martha finally got the musicians to cool it, he took a position on the staircase, with Kate and Harvey down one riser, the guests assembled at the bottom. "Let us all join hands," he said, "in a chain of human interrelationships."

Kate took Harvey's arm in hers and wrapped her fingers warmly around his Pulsar.

"Fellow beings," Thurston said resonantly, "we've come together at this point in time to lend Kate and Harry, here, peer group support while they reaffirm their marriage vows.

"Although Kate and Harry here are already married, in the *legalistic* sense, they've chosen to share with us food and wine and nurturing and community while they celebrate their mutual willingness to give each other space to grow. Their organic union under the cosmos."

"Harvey," Kate hissed at Thurston. "It's *Harvey*."

Thurston turned to her. "Kate," he said, "will you tell us all just where you're coming from?"

Kate was now awash in tears and worried about her contact lenses. "Well," she choked out, somewhat rattled, "I just want to tell Harvey *openly*, I still think he's *número uno*. Commitmentwise. In the human journey."

"Will you tell us what's in *your* heart, Harry?" Thurston socked Harvey on the shoulder in a dynamic but unstructured way and almost knocked him off the steps, so that Harvey clutched unsteadily at Kate. He heard his own voice through a Valium haze.

"Kate," he said, "who loves ya, baby?"

"I can't *stand* it," Martha cried, sobbing loudly on Brian's shoulder. "God, it's just so *nostalgic*, you know?"

"Kate and Harry," Thurston intoned, smiling at them beatifically, "I now pronounce you cojoined persons." He signaled

[318]

that they could break the chain and led the guests in a round of applause, during which Jerry from the car pool whistled piercingly through his teeth.

Shortly afterward Kate and Harvey ran down the steps of Falkirk in a shower of brown rice, headed for a weekend at Sea Ranch. Kate paused at the end of the walk and looked back at the old Victorian mansion. Lights were blazing in the windows, Martha's friend was cooking on the Moog again, and on the porch a knot of people had gathered around Spenser and Spenser's briefcase.

"I kind of blew it," she said to Harvey. "I meant to recite this quote, you know? That Lorca number that Martha did when she got married up on Tam."

"It's not the goal, it's the human journey." Harvey wondered serenely where he'd left the Volvo. "Listen, you're gonna have to drive. I think I took my six-o'clock twice."

"Great. That *tears* it," Kate said, exasperated. "I *can't* drive. I lost a contact lens. We can't go back to the wedding, that's tacky. I mean, wow, what are we gonna *do?*"

Harvey rocked gently back and forth in his Earth Shoes. "Hang loose?" he suggested vaguely.

More Big Bestsellers from SIGNET

☐ **BLOCK BUSTER** by Stephen Barley. (# E8111—$2.25)*

☐ **THE MESSENGER** by Mona Williams. (# J8012—$1.95)

☐ **LOVING SOMEONE GAY** by Don Clark. (# E8593—$2.25)

☐ **FEAR OF FLYING** by Erica Jong. (# E7970—$2.25)

☐ **HOW TO SAVE YOUR OWN LIFE** by Erica Jong.
(# E7959—$2.50)*

☐ **HARVEST OF DESIRE** by Rochelle Larkin.
(# E8183—$2.25)

☐ **MISTRESS OF DESIRE** by Rochelle Larkin.
(# E7964—$2.25)*

☐ **THE FIRES OF GLENLOCHY** by Constance Heaven.
(# E7452—$1.75)

☐ **A PLACE OF STONES** by Constance Heaven.
(# W7046—$1.50)

☐ **THE QUEEN AND THE GYPSY** by Constance Heaven.
(# J7965—$1.95)

☐ **TORCH SONG** by Anne Roiphe. (# J7901—$1.95)

☐ **OPERATION URANIUM SHIP** by Dennis Elsenberg, Eli
Landau, and Menahem Portugall. (# E8001—$1.75)

☐ **NIXON VS. NIXON** by David Abrahamsen.
(# E7902—$2.25)

☐ **ISLAND OF THE WINDS** by Athena Dallas-Damis.
(# J7905—$1.95)

☐ **CARRIE** by Stephen King. (# J7280—$1.95)

☐ **'SALEM'S LOT** by Stephen King. (# E8000—$2.25)

☐ **THE SHINING** by Stephen King. (# E7872—$2.50)

☐ **OAKHURST** by Walter Reed Johnson. (# J7874—$1.95)

☐ **COMA** by Robin Cook. (# E8202—$2.50)

☐ **THE YEAR OF THE INTERN** by Robin Cook.
(# E7674—$1.75)

* Price slightly higher in Canada

Have You Read These Bestsellers from SIGNET?

- [ ] **FRENCH KISS by Mark Logan.** (#J7876—$1.95)
- [ ] **CARIBEE by Christopher Nicole.** (#J7945—$1.95)
- [ ] **THE DEVIL'S OWN by Christopher Nicole.**
  (#J7256—$1.95)
- [ ] **MISTRESS OF DARKNESS by Christopher Nicole.**
  (#J7782—$1.95)
- [ ] **DESIRES OF THY HEART by Joan Carroll Cruz.**
  (#J7738—$1.95)
- [ ] **CALDO LARGO by Earl Thompson.** (#E7737—$2.25)
- [ ] **A GARDEN OF SAND by Earl Thompson.** (#E8039—$2.50)
- [ ] **TATTOO by Earl Thompson.** (#E8038—$2.50)
- [ ] **THE ACCURSED by Paul Boorstin.** (#E7745—$1.75)
- [ ] **THE RICH ARE WITH YOU ALWAYS by Malcolm Macdonald.**
  (#E7682—$2.25)
- [ ] **THE WORLD FROM ROUGH STONES by Malcolm Macdonald.**
  (#J6891—$1.95)
- [ ] **THE FRENCH BRIDE by Evelyn Anthony.** (#J7683—$1.95)
- [ ] **TELL ME EVERYTHING by Marie Brenner.**
  (#J7685—$1.95)
- [ ] **ALYX by Lolah Burford.** (#J7640—$1.95)
- [ ] **MAC LYON by Lolah Burford.** (#J7773—$1.95)

THE NEW AMERICAN LIBRARY, INC.,
P.O. Box 999, Bergenfield, New Jersey 07621

Please send me the SIGNET BOOKS I have checked above. I am enclosing
$_____ (please add 50¢ to this order to cover postage and handling).
Send check or money order—no cash or C.O.D.'s. Prices and numbers are
subject to change without notice.

Name _____

Address _____

City_____ State_____ Zip Code_____

Allow at least 4 weeks for delivery
This offer is subject to withdrawal without notice.

IN 1918 AMERICA FACED AN ENERGY CRISIS

UNCLE SAM NEEDS THAT EXTRA SHOVELFUL

Help Uncle Sam to Win the War

UNITED STATES FUEL ADMINISTRATION

An icy winter gripped the nation. Frozen harbors blocked the movement of coal. Businesses and factories closed. Homes went without heat Prices skyrocketed. It was America's first energy crisis now long since forgotten, like the winter of '76-'77 and the oil embargo of '73-'74. Unfortunately, forgetting a crisis doesn't solve the problems that cause it. Today, the country is relying too heavily on foreign oil. That reliance is costing us over $40 billion dollars a year. Unless we conserve, the world will soon run out of oil, if we don't run out of money first. So the crises of the past may be forgotten, but the energy problems of today and tomorrow remain to be solved. The best solution is the simplest: conservation. It's something every American can do.

ENERGY CONSERVATION -
IT'S YOUR CHANCE TO SAVE, AMERICA
Department of Energy, Washington, D.C.

A PUBLIC SERVICE MESSAGE FROM NEW AMERICAN LIBRARY, INC.